D1101205

WITHDRAWN
SHETLAND LIBRARY
91157560

RIDERS OF THE SHADOWLANDS

RIDERS OF THE SHADOWLANDS

H. A. DeRosso

GUNSMOKE

First published in the US by Five Star

This hardback edition 2012
by AudioGO Ltd
by arrangement with
Golden West Literary Agency

ISBN 978 1 458 8719 7

Acknowledgements may be found on page 229.

British Library Cataloguing in Publication Data available.

Printed and bound in Great Britain by
MPG Books Group Limited

TABLE OF CONTENTS

Foreword

Henry Andrew DeRosso (1917–1960) was the first successful writer of *noir* Westerns — stories and novels of visceral, often existential, content whose characters live, struggle, and die in a suitably desolate, mythical landscape. Like the fiction of suspense writer Cornell Woolrich, DeRosso's work, while sometimes crude and formulaic, has a powerful narrative drive that combines violent action with raw, elemental emotions — love, hate, desire, loneliness, fear, pain, and a pervasive sense of melancholy. One doesn't so much read a DeRosso story as experience it. Even at its most conventional, his work has a depth of feeling and an understanding of the darker side of the human condition that are lacking in the more polished efforts of his peers.

Nearly all of DeRosso's relatively short lifetime was spent in the northern Wisconsin iron-mining town of Hurley, where he was born and where he lived and wrote in solitude. His first stories were penned while he was still in high school; a total of seventy-nine manuscripts were rejected, by his own count, before the eightieth was bought and published in Street & Smith's *Western Story Magazine* in 1941. Over the ensuing twenty years he supported himself mainly as a writer of fiction: more than two hundred and fifty published short stories, novelettes and short novels (most of them Westerns), and four full-length Western novels. (Two additional novels and a dozen or so shorter works were published posthumously. Several others, both short and long, remain unpublished to the present.) He was at the peak of his talent, refining and expanding his abilities and producing some of his best fiction, when ill health befell him and, in October of 1960, a shotgun blast ended his life. It is ironic that such an abrupt and tragic end would come to a man whose fictional creations so often died in a similarly violent fashion.

RIDERS OF THE SHADOWLANDS is the second collection of DeRosso's stories to appear as a Five-Star Western. The first, UNDER THE BURNING SUN (1997), contained a dozen selections and in my Foreword there is a more in-depth analysis of his life and career.

The nine short stories and one short novel in these pages are equally representative of his Western magazine fiction, both chronologically and thematically. As was the case with the stories in the previous collection, those in the present volume were carefully edited. DeRosso's primary weaknesses as a fictioneer were stating and restating the obvious and overburdening his prose with superfluous introspection and repetitive descriptions of hammering hearts, wrathful grimaces, and breath-clogged throats. It may be that he indulged in these excesses with at least some awareness. Pulp writers were paid by the word, and for the most part minimally so. Almost all the editing was in the form of deletions; virtually no rewriting was done, and no changes of any kind were made in plot, character delineation, or thematic statement.

"Killer" first appeared in *Gunsmoke*, a short-lived 1953 magazine devoted to Western stories of the same hard-boiled slant as the crime stories in its sister publication, *Manhunt*. No more hard-edged tale than this one saw print in either of *Gunsmoke*'s two issues. Its theme of personal redemption through hardship was one used often by DeRosso, but seldom more forcefully. In tone, mood, character, theme, and setting, this grim account of a retired sheriff and the code of honor that drives him into a showdown with an escaped convict in the Southwestern shadowlands — here called the Diablos — is a quintessential DeRosso *noir* vision.

Festering hatred with the overpowering need to redress past wrongs was another of DeRosso's compulsive themes. In many such stories by him, savagery and bloodshed were the final outcome. "The Ways of Vengeance" has a different resolution — brought about by the protagonist's interaction with an old man and a little girl — that makes it one of the author's most poignant and satisfying set-pieces.

Deceptively simple in plot and telling, "Fear in the Saddle" portrays a veteran rodeo rider named Travis, seeking to drive out personal demons and regain his self-respect by breaking a wild horse. The bitter conflict between man and animal, suspenseful as it is, is only one element that makes the tale successful; it also has much to say about the nature of fear, and what DeRosso perceived as the ultimate futility of human strife.

Only a handful of his stories saw print in the so-called "better" magazines. His fiction was too grim, the prose too mannered and disturbingly emotional, and the subject matter too conventional to find much favor with other than pulp-magazine editors. One two-part serial, "Under the Burning Sky," which appeared in *Collier's* in 1953, and three shorts published in *Argosy* in the 'Fifties were his only sales to the higher-paying markets. "The Return of the Arapaho Kid" is arguably the best of the trio that graced the pages of *Argosy*, one of the top male-oriented slicks of the period. Despite a familiar plot involving a planned hold-up at an isolated desert stage station, its memorable characters and healthy measure of pathos lift it above the average.

The "Witch" is a Mimbreño Apache girl, Lahneen, who has been cast out from her tribe for saving the life of an owl, an Apache symbol of misfortune. Her life is in turn saved by Les Nathan, a young cowhand on the run for killing a rancher's son in a cattle war. Lahneen's prediction that Nathan will die "before too many sleeps" and her subsequent dogging of his trail add both conflict and suspense to his attempts to elude his pursuers across the obsessive and oppressive shadowlands.

Of DeRosso's more than two hundred and fifty published stories, some forty were written for the mystery and detective magazines — all but a few, skillful blendings of the Western and the crime tale in a contemporary setting. "Dark Purpose" is one such amalgam, offering *noir* variations on both the themes of the eternal triangle and a posse hunting a fugitive. Its background, as in most of DeRosso's modern yarns, is the rugged wilderness of northern Wisconsin. Yet it could just as easily have taken place in similar country in any of the Far West states, and in the 19th rather than the 20th Century.

"The Happy Death" is a strikingly atypical yarn written late in DeRosso's career and published posthumously. The story of a Mexican family living on a large modern ranch, its patriarch who is given to "dying" on a regular basis, and the method he devises to help his *patrón* out of trouble comprise a marked stylistic departure and show a nascent flair for sly humor. The humor, however, has a sardonic bite, and there is a dark undercurrent that runs throughout, making the tale consistent with DeRosso's world-view. There may be such a thing as a "happy death," he seems to be saying here, but it is not without its price — and it may well be all there is for any of us to hope for.

"Bad Blood" tells of a badlands town consumed by hate

for a local cattle baron and his men, a cowhand turned sheriff plagued by the suspicion that he hanged an innocent man, and the efforts of the lawman and his deputy to ferret out the truth and end the trouble. Treachery and deceit lie at the heart of this tale, and the dénouement is yet another affirmation of DeRosso's existential outlook.

As has been noted, his favorite settings were the mythologized desert country of the Southwest and the wilderness region of his home state. "Endless Trail" is one of his few departures from these backgrounds, and his only story to take place in the Far North. Set in Alaska at the time of the 1902 Gold Rush, it is the saga of an aging town-tamer who longs finally to settle down and live a peaceful married life — a goal threatened by circumstances and his own private devils. DeRosso understood the tormented soul better than any Western writer past or present, and his depiction of Dan Burkett's in this story is particularly incisive.

First published in *Complete Western Book Magazine* in 1950, "Riders of the Shadowlands" is a long, action-filled pulp yarn about a Cattle Association detective, Gatewood, on the trail of rustlers and his own salvation in the Doloritas — another name for that landscape, half-real and half-nightmare, that was uniquely DeRosso's own. Its elements of loneliness, personal quest, disillusionment, loss, and redemption only at great cost overshadow its conventional plotline. Gatewood, like Dan Harland, the leading character in DeRosso's best novel, *.44*, published by Lion Books in 1953 and reissued by Leisure Books in 1997, and like so many of his other protagonists is a haunted dreamer who is tortured by self-doubt and a feeling of alienation, and driven by forces beyond his ken that seem to be leading him inexorably to the brink of destruction.

H. A. DeRosso knew these men well, and portrayed them so convincingly, because in essence he was one of them — a rider of the shadowlands.

Bill Pronzini
Petaluma, California

Killer

I

It was the middle of the morning, when the rider topped the rise and started down the road to Baxter's ranch. Baxter was down in a corral, teaching a colt to respond to the bit, when the horseman appeared. Baxter stopped his work and came out of the corral.

He went over to the windmill and had a drink, and then his eyes sought the rider again. The land was flat and open here, making it possible to see a long way. The rider was nearer, but he was still unrecognizable. There seemed to be something portentous in the way he came, with deliberateness and lack of hurry.

Baxter leaned against the edge of the tank and watched. He was a tall, lean man with a brown, creased face. His lips were parted a little with the intensity of his stare, thus revealing the startling whiteness of his teeth. His eyes were a shade between green and gray, and he had a long nose that was hooked a little at the bridge. His gaunt cheeks made tiny hollows on either side of his face.

He was dressed in blue Levi's and a tan denim shirt that had small spots of wetness under the armpits and in the small of the back. He wore the Levi's with a wide cuff that revealed the lower half of plain black boots that were beginning to show wear. His spurs were plain steel affairs with small rowels. His hat was a high-crowned Stetson, creased in the front and with the brim curled up at the sides.

Baxter built a smoke and watched the rider come on. The horseman grew as he approached and eventually recognition came to Baxter. The rider was Sheriff Mike McCall.

McCall spied Baxter at the tank and turned his roan that way. He rode the horse up to the water, and then dismounted. There was dust on McCall's clothing, and he brushed some of this off before he took a drink.

Then he said: "Hello, Dan."

Dan Baxter nodded. He had been sheriff of Doña Luz county before McCall. Two years ago he had retired to devote all his time to ranching, and Mike McCall had been elected. McCall was a good man, Baxter thought.

Baxter's eyes narrowed as they studied the sheriff. Mike McCall was a stocky man of medium height. He was in his early forties. He had a wide face marked by two long dimples and a pair of hard, gray eyes. Today he looked rather grim.

Baxter glanced from McCall's face to the man's weapons. The black handle of a .45 Colt jutted out of McCall's holster, and every loop of this belt was filled with shells. Above this belt, McCall wore another, this one studded with .44-40s for the Winchester that he carried in his saddle scabbard. A chill sense of foreboding settled between Baxter's shoulder blades.

McCall took out the makings and built himself a cigarette with care. He proffered the Bull Durham to Baxter, but Baxter showed him what he had left of his smoke, and so McCall put the tobacco sack back in a shirt pocket. He struck a match and lit his smoke and took a deep inhalation. When he let it out, he did so with an audible, lingering sigh.

Mike McCall stared down at the cigarette in his fingers and said: "Jesse Olivera broke out of the pen, Dan."

"When did you find out?"

"The wire came this morning. Olivera broke out early last night, but they didn't let me know until they were sure he was heading this way."

"This way?" Baxter echoed.

"Where else?"

Yes, Baxter thought, *where else?* For five years he had been expecting this day. As time wore on, he had begun to forget a little. The reality of it had faded until it was almost like the memory of a bad dream, but the remembrance had never gone completely. It was a thing that had to be, Baxter thought. It had an inevitability as certain as death.

He became aware that McCall was staring intently at him. However, Baxter kept staring out over the land but never quite seeing it. He was seeing only the image of Jesse Olivera.

"I thought I'd stop by and let you know," McCall said after a while.

"Thanks, Mike."

"Keep your eyes peeled."

"I'll do that."

McCall took a last puff on his smoke and ground it out under his heel. "Well, I've got to get going."

"Where you headed?"

"The Diablos." McCall paused. "That's where Olivera was headed the last time he was seen."

"No posse?"

McCall shrugged. "Olivera's one man," he said. "Would you have taken a posse?"

Baxter smiled faintly and shook his head.

Saddle leather creaked as McCall swung up into the kak. He settled himself in the seat. His lips parted a little as though he were going to say something, but then he decided against it. He touched the roan with the spurs.

Baxter said: " 'Luck, Mike."

McCall acknowledged this with a slight rise of his right hand. Then the roan was moving away. It circled the buildings and then struck out across the land in a direct line for the Diablos. McCall rode hunched forward. He never looked back.

Baxter stood a while by the tank, lost in thought. His thinking was mostly of the old days and of how at one time the enforcement of the law had meant everything to him. It had been more than a job or a career with him. It had almost been a sacred dedication to duty.

In those days, he had thought that he would never voluntarily give up the sheriff's job. That had been before the capture and arrest of Jesse Olivera. Afterward, the job began to pall on Baxter, and eventually he had decided not to run for reëlection. He gave the excuse that he had bought a ranch and that he had recently married, but in the privacy of his own mind he knew it was something more than that. It was something he did not like to think about.

He had known this day would come. He had known it as surely and inevitably as night follows day. He had known that stone walls and steel bars would not hold Jesse Olivera, not with what Olivera had in mind. Now that it had happened, Baxter, somehow, felt relieved.

It did not take Baxter long to decide what to do. He was of the frontier, and he lived by a code. The code was harsh and grim and even brutal at times, but it was the only way of life Dan Baxter knew. It was also the way of life for Jesse Olivera. He owed something to the man, Baxter thought. He would give it to Olivera.

Baxter went back to the breaking corral and unsaddled the colt. Then he saddled a buckskin, which was his favorite mount, and led the animal up to the house.

When he came through the door, Penny, his wife, said: "What did Mike McCall want?"

Baxter scarcely heard her. His mind was on other things. She repeated the question.

Baxter collected himself enough to answer her. "He just stopped to water his horse, Penny."

He took his belt and holstered .44 down from a peg on the wall. Breaking open a fresh box of cartridges, he filled the empty loops. Then he buckled the belt about his waist. After that, he picked up his Winchester in its saddle boot.

"What's up, Dan?" Penny asked. There was a little apprehension in her tone.

Baxter knew he had to tell her something. He could not tell her the truth, because she would not understand. Even he did not understand it fully. He searched for words and found none.

Penny placed herself in front of him so that he could not go to the door. She took his arms in her hands and tilted her head back to study his face better. He tried a smile, hoping to reassure her with it, but it did not quite come off.

"Where are you going?" she asked. "What are you going to do?"

He stared at her, helpless for words. She was a very pretty woman, he thought, and he considered himself fortunate, having her for a wife. The top of her blonde head reached to his chin. With her head dropped back, he could see the troubled look in her blue eyes. She had long, thin lips and a smooth, round face. Seeing her like this made him remember the many times he'd had her in his arms and reminded him, poignantly, that perhaps he might never hold her again.

"McCall told you something," she said, when he did not speak. He could feel the pressure of her fingers against his flesh. "What was it, Dan?"

He supposed she had to know. He shrugged and said, looking away from her: "Jesse Olivera broke out of the pen. He's up in the Diablos."

Her breath made a sharp sound as she sucked it in. She knew about him and Olivera, but she did not understand exactly how it was and how it had to be. She could never understand a thing like that.

"Where are you going, then?" she asked.

He told her as much as he would ever tell her. "Into the Diablos."

"No," she said. He saw the sudden fear constrict the corners of her mouth. "You can't go there. You mustn't. You know that Olivera has sworn to kill you."

Baxter shrugged. He said nothing. He just didn't know the words to express what he felt inside.

"Let McCall do it alone," she begged. "If he needs help, let him find someone else."

"I'm not going with McCall. I'm going alone."

"Alone?" she echoed, as if she could not believe what she had heard. "Why alone?"

"I have to."

He broke her grip on him, gently, and went over and began getting a pack of food together. She came with him. She kept trying to turn him around so that he would have to look at her, but he kept his face averted.

"Dan," she cried, "this doesn't make sense. You've got to be careful. You've got to stay here where Olivera can't get to you."

"If he got out of the pen, he can get here."

"Maybe McCall will take him. Isn't that what he's going into the Diablos for?"

"Maybe McCall won't be able to take him."

"But what can you do? What can you do alone? He'll kill you, Dan. He'll kill you."

She started to cry now. It was the first time he had seen her this way. Nothing could deter him, not even this woman whom he loved dearly.

Gently, he forced her hands away from her face. He put a finger under her chin and tilted it. Tears were channeling down her cheeks.

"Look, Penny," he said, "it's something I've got to do. It's something I owe to Olivera. That's the only way I can put it. I know you don't understand, but that's the way it is."

"It wasn't your fault," she said. "You were only doing your job. You don't owe Olivera anything. Please don't go into the Diablos."

"I've got to," he said with a sigh. "I've got to."

II

He did not build a fire that night. It was a chance he could not take. He wrapped himself up in his blankets and lay on the cold ground. For supper he'd had cold biscuits that he'd taken with him and jerky.

He was in the Diablos. Not very deep perhaps, but he was in them. In the darkness he could sense the looming of the high, naked peaks all around him. Stars glittered overhead. All about there was the silence of the mountains, awesome and mysterious and forbidding. The only sounds he heard were the fretful stirrings of his buckskin as it moved around at the end of its picket rope.

Baxter lay there in his blankets and tried to sleep. He would close his eyes and concentrate on dropping off, but that never worked. It only brought the memory more vividly to his mind. He tried fighting it at first, but then he realized the futility of this.

He lay there with his eyes wide open now, remembering. He had gone to arrest Jesse Olivera on a charge of rustling. It had been a night, something like this, that he'd ridden up to Olivera's place.

He dismounted and called out Olivera's name. Olivera replied with a gunshot. Baxter took cover. He called out to Olivera to surrender. Olivera replied with defiance and more gunshots. So Baxter settled down to wait it out.

The stars were out, and they gave a little light. It was possible to distinguish shadows, although the exact nature of them was not too apparent. It was under these conditions that Olivera made a break for it.

Two of them burst from the house together, and on the instant Baxter did not stop to think. He called out a warning, and the blaring of a gun answered him. The two were making for a corral.

Baxter laid down his reply with his .44. He emptied the weapon, and then it was over, except for the echoes that were still rolling in the far distance. Baxter reloaded, and then he went in cautiously to see what had been done.

One of them was dead. At first, Baxter thought this was a rather slim boy, but then, bending down, he got a look at long hair fanned out, and the realization was like a hard blow in the stomach. This was a woman dressed in men's clothing. This was María Olivera, Jesse Olivera's wife.

Olivera still lived. He was faint with shock and the pain of his wound, but he came to enough to try to bring up his gun. Baxter knocked it out of his hand. Olivera dragged himself on the ground until he was next to his dead wife. He felt her dead face and caressed her hair. He did not cry. He dipped a finger in the blood of his dead wife and drew a cross on his forehead. Then he looked up at Baxter.

"I will kill you one day," said Olivera. "I swear I will kill you. In the blood of my María I swear it. . . ."

It was the remembrance of this that did not let Baxter sleep. He lay there, staring wide-eyed at the night. The air was cold, but beads of sweat coated Baxter's brow.

The three riders appeared early the next morning. Patches of shadow still clung to the mountainsides because the sun was not yet high enough. Sage and manzanita huddled lonesomely. There was stillness everywhere except for the sounds the buckskin made.

The horse topped a hill, and there below him Baxter spied the riders. They spotted him, too, and they reined in their mounts, and for a while they sat there, staring up at him. He knew them, and they knew him.

After a while, Baxter sent the buckskin down the slope. The three waited for him. When he rode up, two of the riders nodded their greetings. The third one spoke.

"Hello, Dan," he said.

"Hello, George."

The one who had spoken was George Chamberlain. He was about Baxter's age, thirty-four. Chamberlain was a tall, tawny man with a yellow mustache drooping down around the corners of his mouth. His eyes also held a hint of yellow color, and they seemed forever withdrawn and wary.

Baxter noted the filled shell belt about Chamberlain's waist and the butt of a carbine sticking out of a saddle boot. Baxter looked then at Chamberlain's companions and noted that they, too, were heavily armed. It seemed that everyone who rode into the Diablos now was overloaded with hardware, Baxter thought grimly.

Those cautious eyes of Chamberlain studied Baxter carefully. "You alone?" asked Chamberlain.

Baxter nodded.

Chamberlain took out a sack and began to build a cigarette. Baxter could feel the other two studying him intently. He turned his head and gave each of them a cool, hard appraisal. These were not enemies, but he had never admired them, either, and this feeling was reciprocated.

Len Yates was a small, slight man, quick in his movements, and with a pair of sly eyes that were never still. A bristle of beard covered his cheeks and chin, and one side of his face bulged from a healthy chew. He sat in his kak, hands folded over the horn, eyes constantly darting from Baxter to the horizon and then back to Baxter again. At his hips, Yates wore a pair of tied-down .45s.

Frank Parnell was a short, gross man with a large belly that overflowed the top of his trousers. He was dark, and his skin had an oily tint, so that he constantly appeared ready to break out in a sweat. His black eyes seemed set deep in thick pouches of fat, and they were keen and piercing. Parnell appeared lazy in his movements, but this was deceptive. The shell belt around his ample waist supported a holstered Remington .44-40.

Chamberlain had his cigarette built now, and he lit it and then exhaled a cloud of smoke. "I suppose you've heard about Olivera."

"I have."

Chamberlain kept looking at the smoke in his hand. "How come you're in the Diablos, then?"

Baxter said nothing. There really was nothing to say.

Chamberlain said: "Don't you know that Olivera is supposed to be up here?"

"Mike McCall told me."

"Oh?" said Chamberlain. "Are you going to join McCall?"

"I'm not joining anybody."

Chamberlain took a deep drag on his smoke and exhaled slowly. He appeared to be thinking of something. After a pause, he said: "You don't make sense, Dan."

"Why don't I?"

Chamberlain lifted his shoulders in a shrug and made a small mouth. "You've got everything to lose and nothing to gain by going it alone. Just what do you have in mind?"

"Nothing that is any of your business."

Chamberlain flushed and started to come up in the stirrups, but then he checked himself. He settled back in his kak, his face taut.

"One of these days you're going too far, Dan," he said angrily.

"When I do, you better have your two boys with you. You'll probably need them."

Len Yates spat a curse. His right hand came off the saddle horn and took up a post next to the handle of a .45. Frank Parnell started to grin. It was the grin of a panther.

Chamberlain took a deep breath. "Look, Dan," he said, "I'm not trying to pick a fight with you. You're on edge, and I can understand why. When you come to think of it, we're both in the same cavvy. We both want Olivera dead."

"Who said I want him dead?"

"What else would you want him? You know he'll kill you the first chance he gets. Isn't that what you came up here for? To beat him to it?"

Baxter did not answer. The futility of trying to explain came over him again.

Chamberlain went on: "Why don't you throw in with us, Dan? You know the Diablos better than we do. We'll get

Olivera for sure then. All I want is to be the one to put the slug in him that kills him. Or, if we take him alive, I want to be the one to whip the horse out from under him, when we hang him. Is it a deal?"

Baxter shook his head. "I'm going it alone," he said.

Chamberlain's face darkened. He gave a savage wrench to the lines that swung his sorrel up against Baxter's buckskin. "Listen to me. Olivera's my meat. I mean to get him, one way or another. If McCall gets him before I do, I'm taking him away from McCall. He killed my brother Billy. I'll get Olivera for that, if it's the last thing I ever do on this earth."

"Olivera killed Billy in a fair fight," said Baxter. "Billy started it, and Olivera killed him in self-defense. He was acquitted in court. I was sheriff at the time. Don't you remember?"

"I remember," said Chamberlain heavily. "I remember, all right. I remember it was you who kept me from squaring with Olivera. I've remembered that for over five years. So keep out of my way, Dan. If you're not hankering to die, keep out of my way!"

III

The mountains seemed somber and lonely. There was something sinister in all this desolation, in all this waste. The lack of any living thing heightened the feeling of depression that had settled over Baxter. When once he saw a vulture floating up against the sky, he welcomed the sight. He was that low right now.

It was after the middle of the day that it abruptly came to Baxter that he was not alone. It came as a crawling sensation that seemed to reach every part of his body. He reined in the buckskin and looked around, but there was nothing to see except the emptiness of the land. The peaks towered naked and mighty. There were sage and mesquite here on the valley floor, and the rising and dipping of the hills. Clumps of jackpine clung to the mountain walls. This was all that he saw, but the certainty lived in him that there was more.

He rode the buckskin to the top of a hill. Even though this skylighted him, it gave him a vantage point to scan the country from. He squinted his eyes and studied the land carefully. It threw its emptiness back at him, mockingly. But he knew something was out there.

He sent the buckskin down the other slope of the hill and then started across the valley. He thought of Mike McCall, and then of Chamberlain and Yates and Parnell, but they would be open about it. They would not trail him on the sly.

That left only Jesse Olivera.

The skin crawled at the back of Baxter's neck. For a few moments, he told himself, he had been a fool to have come up here into the Diablos. He should have stayed on his ranch and waited for Olivera to come to him. But Baxter had the feeling that Olivera would never get out of these mountains alive.

He rode the buckskin to another hilltop and reined in and studied the country once more. Only the inanimateness of the terrain showed. Not even a vulture was in the sky now.

He rode on. He came to a stretch of ground littered with huge slabs of rock, the monuments of some primeval upheaval. The earth was hard here; the buckskin left hardly a trace of its passing. Baxter rode through here, and then he sent the buckskin up a steep slope. The buckskin worked hard, but it got up the slope, and here Baxter halted it and dismounted.

He saw where he could climb up to a shelf that would give him a commanding view of the land below. He tied the buckskin to a jackpine, and then, taking his Winchester, he climbed up to the shelf. He was quite high here. The undulations of the land stretched out below him.

Baxter stared until his eyes ached, and then he stared some more. He thought once that he glimpsed a movement. However, it was so fleeting that he could not pin it down. It could have been the glinting of the sun off a piece of quartz — or off a blued gun barrel.

He waited with the sun burning on his back. He waited with sweat trickling down the sides of his face and dripping off his chin. He waited until he was sure no one would come, and then he went on waiting. All the while he could hear the slow, measured beating of his heart against the ground.

Frustration finally brought him down from the shelf. Mounting his buckskin, he rode off on his search again. He was not yet quite sure what he had in mind. He wanted to find Olivera, but beyond that he was uncertain.

Again the feeling that he was not alone came to Baxter. He could not understand this intuition. It made him uneasy, and then it started a slow swirl of wrath building up in him. If he was going to let it get him like this, he should turn around and go home. He knew, however, that he would never do that. The thing was too compelling within him.

He topped a hill and, hipping around in the saddle, gave a look down his back trail. This time he spied someone. This was not a figment of his imagination. That was a horseman back there. It was Mike McCall.

The sheriff rode up with a puzzled frown on his face. He

looked Baxter carefully up and down, and then frowned again.

"I didn't think I'd see you up here, Dan," the sheriff said.

"Well, I'm here," said Baxter. His tone was hard. He was feeling nettled and mean inside.

McCall shifted his weight a little more comfortably in the kak. His face looked drawn and tired. A red beard stubble sprinkled his cheeks and throat. His clothing was soiled with dust and sweat. Baxter supposed he didn't look any better. This matter was a strain on him, also.

McCall raised a hand and scratched the stubble on his chin. His eyes held a pensive glint. "What's on your mind, Dan?"

Baxter showed a brief, mirthless grin. "I'm just out for a ride in the sun."

"Let's not get funny about it," McCall said with a small show of irritation. "For some reason you want Olivera."

"Why should I want Olivera?"

"That's why I'm asking. There's no reason for it. It isn't that you've got something to square with the man. It's the other way around. Yet, here you are, riding around for all the world like you're giving Olivera a crack at you. It doesn't make sense."

Baxter said nothing.

McCall's stare was hard and contemplative. "Why do you want to kill Olivera?"

"What makes you think I want to kill him?"

"What other reason would you have for coming up here? You know Olivera will throw down on you the minute he spots you."

Baxter said nothing. He was listening to the dull, heavy beating of his heart. His mind, for a moment, was on a distant memory.

"There's one way I've got it figured out," McCall went on after a pause. "Maybe you don't like to sit around on your hands and wait. Maybe you figure on carrying the fight to Olivera, to catch him off balance that way. But this still isn't like you, Dan. You're not a killer."

Baxter sat, thinking now of his wife, Penny, and a great longing came over him. It wasn't fair to her, he told himself, but then he put the consideration from him. The thing gnawing at his mind allowed for no such considerations.

McCall sighed. "Olivera will be taken care of, Dan. I won't give up until I've got him. Go on home, won't you?"

"Have you spotted any sign of him?" asked Baxter.

"I was following a set of tracks that were following yours," said McCall, "but then they faded out. It was like someone had seen me coming. Olivera's as cunning as an Injun, you know."

"You see anything else?"

"You mean Chamberlain?"

Baxter nodded.

McCall said: "I saw George and his boys. They didn't see me, though. I thought it best to keep out of their sight." He directed a sharp glance at Baxter. "You know what will happen to Olivera, if they get to him before I do."

"That's why I want to reach Olivera first," said Baxter.

"And I want to get to Olivera first because I want to take him alive."

"Do you think you can?"

"At least, I'll try," said McCall with a trace of anger. "That's more than you and Chamberlain can say."

Baxter did not comment. He was thinking that, strange as it was, he almost experienced a kinship with Jesse Olivera. It was as though he were being drawn irresistibly toward the man.

McCall was staring at him keenly. After a while, the sheriff said: "How about joining me, Dan?"

Baxter shook his head.

"Then you really mean to kill Olivera?"

"Let's not talk about it any more," said Baxter tiredly. "You just wouldn't understand. . . ."

IV

Baxter sat there in his saddle, watching Sheriff Mike McCall ride away. McCall rode around the shoulder of a hill and was gone from sight, and Baxter was alone again. Once more he had only his thoughts for company.

He recalled what McCall had said about following the tracks of someone who had been following Baxter. He had not imagined something, after all. It had really been Olivera on his back trail. It could have been no one else. The man had been stalking him. Then Olivera had become aware of the presence of McCall and had slipped away. There could no longer be any doubt that he was here in the Diablos. Although this was what he wanted, nevertheless the realization left Baxter rather cold at the pit of his stomach.

Finally, he started the buckskin, taking a direction different from the way McCall had gone. Baxter headed for a notch between two peaks. He stopped often to study his back trail. Nothing out of the way appeared. Only the land was there, forsaken and wasted. Even the uneasiness he had experienced earlier that day had vanished. It was as though he were all alone in a great, forgotten universe of his own.

He gained the notch at sundown. He stopped and made another cold, dry camp. Now that Olivera knew he was here in the Diablos, Baxter could risk a fire even less.

He lay awake a long time, staring off into the night. His ears strained for any alien sounds, but the only noises he heard were those made by the picketed buckskin. This was not particularly reassuring. Olivera would not be making a racket, if he were creeping in out of the night.

He did not think only of Olivera, however. He thought also of his wife, Penny. It was now on the second night that he really missed her. A feeling of sadness came over Baxter. If he should die — and the chances were fifty-fifty that he would — it would be a terrible blow to her. He began to feel depressed, thinking in this fashion, and angrily he put the thoughts aside. His mind reverted to Olivera. It stayed with Olivera until he finally dropped off.

He awoke with a start, surprised that the sun was up. He came awake with his heart pounding, and he threw a hard, wary look all around, scanning the country for any doubtful signs, but only the emptiness of the land lay in his gaze. At first, he felt relieved, and then a great impatience and irritation came over him. Time was passing. If he was to meet Olivera, it had to be soon. The longer it was delayed, the greater became the possibility that Olivera would meet up with Mike McCall or George Chamberlain and his men. Urgency possessed Baxter now.

He went back the way he'd come, hoping by this to encounter Olivera should the man have picked up his trail again. He rode openly now, taking all the high spots, highlighting himself on the crests of all the hills and ridges for anybody to see who should be watching. Perversely enough, this produced no results.

As the morning mounted, the peaks seemed to leer at him in evil mockery. The emptiness of the land taunted him. A feeling began to torment him, a feeling of futility and despair. There was nothing for him here, the feeling told him; he was on a fruitless hunt. Olivera was not for him. The old obligation would not be settled. Olivera was meant for either McCall or Chamberlain.

Baxter felt full of anger and frustration. He gnashed his teeth and cursed feelingly. He was licked; he might as well quit and go home. It was a foolish impulse that had brought him into the Diablos in the first place.

He was at the lowest point of his spirits when the shots came. On the instant, Baxter froze in his kak. Then he reined in the buckskin sharply and listened.

The shots had not been directed at him. They came from somewhere ahead of him. McCall? Or Chamberlain? Was he too late? Was Olivera already dead?

Then another flurry of shots came. There was something reassuring about them. Evidently, Olivera was not dead or taken yet.

Baxter sent the buckskin ahead. He was all tense and caught up inside. He knew both elation and dread. He still could not decide what the shooting portended. He could see the rim of a cliff ahead. The shooting had come from beyond and below this. Baxter dismounted and tied the buckskin to a mesquite bush. He took his Winchester and went ahead, cautiously, on foot.

As he neared the rim, he dropped first to his knees, and then to his belly and dragged himself along the ground like that. Two more shots rang out, but there seemed to be something desultory and futile in their sound. Baxter was very close to the rim now. His exertions had him breathing hard.

Jackpine was scattered along the rim of the cliff which dropped almost precipitously to the floor of a cañon fifty feet below. Baxter took a lot of care so that he would not reveal himself. He had no idea how it was down below, and he was taking no unnecessary chances.

He wiggled his way through a small clump of jackpine, and this brought him to the lip of the rim. Breath held in his throat, he peered cautiously over the edge of the cliff. Below and a little distance ahead, a man was crouched in the shelter of several slabs of rock. As Baxter watched, the man called out something. The sound of his voice drifted up to Baxter, but it was so faint the words were indistinguishable.

The man was Sheriff Mike McCall.

Looking beyond McCall to the other side of the narrow cañon, Baxter saw where another man was forted up among another smattering of boulders. Was this Olivera? It had to be.

For several moments, Baxter was nagged by indecision. Several alternatives clamored at his brain, each one insisting on its superiority. A trickle of sweat flowed down Baxter's cheeks. A pulse started an insistent throbbing at his temple.

McCall rose up a little behind his rocks for a better look, and the man across the cañon got off a shot. The slug glanced off stone and went whining up the cañon. McCall dropped swiftly behind his shelter. He began shooting again. His only reply was another shot from the man who must be Olivera.

This was a stand-off, Baxter thought. Each man had the other pinned down. If Olivera did not want to surrender, this could go on indefinitely. Perhaps Olivera was waiting for nightfall which would afford him a chance to sneak away.

Baxter thought of George Chamberlain. There was no telling where Chamberlain and Yates and Parnell were. If they should be within hearing distance of the gunfire, they would investigate. If they did that and found Olivera here, he would not live to see the sun go down. It was this consideration that affirmed Baxter's decision.

Sweat was trickling down into his eyes. Angrily, he brushed it away. His heart beat louder than ever. A sneering voice jeered at him, telling him he was a fool to do it this way. He tried not to listen to it, but it drummed at him, relentlessly.

Baxter could see a black horse across the cañon. The animal appeared to be tied to a manzanita. Evidently, this was Olivera's mount.

Baxter poked his Winchester over the rim of the cañon. Chillingly, he realized he was gambling that Olivera would select escape rather than the death of the sheriff. He aimed carefully with the Winchester, and then he began to fire. He bounced the slugs off the rocks all around McCall. He saw McCall go down, burrowing flat against the slab to shield himself.

Baxter kept on firing. He let up once to see how Olivera was reacting, and it was with relief that he saw the man racing for his horse. In this interval, McCall poked his rifle above the rock and snapped off a shot, but Baxter drove him back to cover with two quick shots off the surface of the stone.

By now, Olivera had mounted. He waved an arm in thanks at the rim of the cañon, and then he set spurs to his black. A wry grin twisted Baxter's mouth. There would have been no display of gratitude had Olivera known who it was up here. The black was racing swiftly up the cañon.

Baxter emptied his Winchester, and then he drew back from the cañon's lip. Bullets began to snarl up at the spot he had just vacated. He crawled on hands and knees until he was sure he could not be seen from below. Then he jumped to his feet and ran to the buckskin. He was positive he had not been recognized by Mike McCall.

V

Baxter made another lonely, fireless camp that night. He chewed on some jerky, the extent of his supper. Even had he had a fire, he would not have eaten anything else. He didn't have the appetite.

He felt tired and beaten. All this business of being alone, of being obsessed by a drive and urge that was not completely clear even to himself, had him doubting if he could keep up with it. He wanted peace and rest. He longed more than ever for the embrace of Penny. But he had to pursue his relentless purpose until he had achieved it — or until it brought him to his death.

He dreamed many dreams this night. In one he saw himself as a bloody corpse with Penny, weeping heartbrokenly over him. He came awake with a start, sitting bolt upright, and the sound of crying was still real in his ears. He listened for a long while before it came to him that there was nothing to listen to.

Afterward, he lay down once more and slept. He went on dreaming — twisted, garbled, fantastic dreams. When morning came and he awoke, he felt as tired and beaten as the night before.

He came upon a tiny creek later that morning. Here he paused to rest the buckskin and to re-fill his canteen. He bathed his face in the cool water and splashed some on the back of his neck. The water seemed to revive him. Some of the depression left him.

After the buckskin had drunk its fill and rested, Baxter mounted and rode on. The land was different here. An occasional pine and cedar grew, but these were not dwarfs. They were full-size trees. There was also a little graze, but the land was still void of human habitation.

He followed the creek to its source which was a spring issuing from the fissure in a large wall of rock. Here Baxter paused because the ground was high and afforded him a look at the surrounding area. He glanced around carefully and saw nothing. Then he gave a look at the sky, and up there he saw the vultures.

The buzzards were gathering. There were half a dozen of them, floating around on wide-spread, motionless wings. As Baxter watched, one of them swooped down, disappearing behind an intervening hill, and failed to appear again. After a while, another one banked and started down.

Baxter started the buckskin. He rode up the side of the hill with his heart beating fast and his hand tight about the handle of his gun.

When he topped the hill, the vultures rose with a foul flapping of wings. Baxter instantly saw the man, but from up here he could not tell who it was. Slowly, Baxter sent the buckskin down the slope. He gave a swift search of the surrounding land with wary eyes but beheld nothing. The only living things were him and the buckskin and the vultures, wheeling overhead.

The man lay sprawled on his back with his face turned to one side, away from Baxter. Olivera — the thought sped through Baxter's mind — but this man was too heavy and stocky to be Olivera, unless Olivera had put on a lot of weight in prison. The man's arms were thrown out, and one knee was drawn up in a final reflex of agony. Blood stained the front of his shirt. Blood had also poured out of his mouth to stain one side of his face and to form a small, crimson pool on the ground. His mouth was still slacked open, and his wide-open eyes had the blank, intense stare of death.

The dead man was Frank Parnell.

There was no way to bury Parnell, and besides a deviling urgency possessed Baxter. He rode the buckskin around, studying the many marks in the ground. He followed tracks over another hill, and there he found Parnell's mount, grazing placidly.

Baxter scouted around some more, until he found the tracks of three horses going away. His throat grew dry as he read the implication in this.

Chamberlain must have Olivera. That explained the three horses. They must have cornered him here, and Olivera had killed Parnell before being taken. He must still be alive, or his body would have been left here for the buzzards as Parnell's corpse had been. Chamberlain would have less feeling for Olivera than for one of his own men.

The realization that he might still be alive was not cheering to Baxter. He knew how deeply and thoroughly George Chamberlain could hate. He must have something special in mind for Jesse Olivera.

A need for haste in him, Baxter started out after the tracks. A needling insistence kept telling him he would be too late. He was tempted time and again to abandon caution and send the buckskin on as fast as the animal could run. But Baxter kept a grip on himself. He kept the buckskin moving at a trot that ate up the distance.

Parnell had died in open country where there had been no trees. Baxter remembered Chamberlain's words — *I want to be the one to put the slug in him that kills him. I want to be the one to whip the horse out from under him, when we hang him.* The sense of urgency doubled in Baxter.

The tracks climbed a ridge whose top was studded with pines and cedars. Baxter rode into these, heart apprehensive. He had the feeling that he was nearing the end of his search. These trees were what Chamberlain was seeking. When he found one that suited his purpose, he would stop, and there Olivera would die.

Baxter saw where the horses had stopped beside a tall cedar as though this one had been considered. However, the limbs were too close to the ground, and the three had ridden on. Baxter urged the buckskin on a trifle faster.

He peered ahead, trying to see around and beyond the scattered trees; he stared until his eyes began to ache. Then, through the avenues of the trees, he caught a glimpse of something ahead.

As he advanced, he made out a clearing. To one side in the clearing stood a majestic pine. Its trunk was immense; its lowest limbs were high enough for a horse and rider easily to pass underneath. This was the tree that George Chamberlain had been looking for.

It was easier than Baxter dared to hope. Chamberlain and Yates were so intent on what they were doing, and they were so confident of being alone, that they concentrated only on the job at hand. Contrary to Chamberlain's words of the other day, he was not going to whip a horse from under Olivera. Chamberlain had come up with a much slower and more painful death, although hanging was still the name for it.

There was not much time, Baxter thought, as he circled the edge of the clearing so that he could come in behind Chamberlain and Yates. He moved as fast as he dared. He hoped the buckskin would not make any sudden, sharp noise to warn Chamberlain.

Olivera was not on a horse. He stood on the ground with his hands bound behind his back. A noose was around his neck, the rope had been passed over a limb, and the other end of the rope was dallied around Chamberlain's saddle horn. There was to be no sudden drop, no snapping of the neck. Chamberlain's intent was clear. He would send his horse ahead, just enough to lift Olivera's toes off the ground. A slow, painful strangulation was what Chamberlain had in mind.

Baxter's .44 was in his hand as he rode out of the trees. In his ears Chamberlain's wrathful, hate-ridden words raged.

"How do you like it, Olivera?" Chamberlain was saying as he kneed his horse ahead a little, tightening the rope so that the noose dug into the doomed man's neck. "How do you like the feel of it? Maybe you can tell Billy when you see him in hell."

Len Yates sat on his horse beside Chamberlain. Yates was watching with an avid fascination. Neither man was aware of Baxter, coming up behind them. Chamberlain moved his horse a little more, and Olivera strained up on his toes, his face contorting. Yates's laugh was soft and evil.

Wrath swept over Baxter. He experienced a sudden, heedless urge to open up with his .44, to cut down Chamberlain and Yates without warning. But a thing like this was not in Baxter's nature.

The click as he cocked his .44 was a soft, but perceptible, sound. Both Chamberlain and Yates heard it. They froze in their kaks, their heads thrust up, stiff with alarm.

"Let that rope go, George," Baxter said.

Yates whirled his horse to face Baxter. Yates's right hand was on the ivory handles of one gun. His eyes were hard and his face like an iron mask.

Chamberlain spoke. He still had his back to Baxter, and Olivera was still up on his toes, fighting for breath. "Keep out of this, Dan," said Chamberlain. "I'm warning you. Keep out of this."

"I said let that rope go," snapped Baxter.

Yates started to edge his horse to the side. Baxter swung his gun to cover the fellow. "Hold it, Yates," he growled.

"Don't listen to him, Len," said Chamberlain. "He's only bluffing. He won't shoot to save a dirty rustler and sneaking killer. Don't let him bluff you."

"Does this look like a bluff?" said Baxter. He swung his .44 back and fired. The bullet whipped Chamberlain's hat from his head. He emitted a shout of alarm, and his hand inadvertently released the rope and grabbed for his gun. The dally slipped off the horn, and Olivera dropped to his knees.

Len Yates took this opportunity to draw his gun. Baxter saw it and swung his .44 back and fired. The slug slammed Yates in the chest. A hurt groan ripped out of his throat, his horse shied, and Yates went pitching out of his saddle.

Chamberlain had his gun out now. Baxter jabbed the buckskin with the spurs, and the horse leaped ahead just as Chamberlain fired. The bullet made a wailing whine past Baxter's ear. He was crouched low in the saddle, his .44 thrust out ahead of him. He thumbed off a shot and then another one, swiftly. The first slug took Chamberlain in the breast; the second one drilled his neck. He began to make harsh, garbled sounds, clawing all the while at his throat, and then he plunged headlong to the ground.

VI

Baxter dismounted. His knees felt weak and shaky, and there was a fluttering in his stomach, but the sensation passed quickly enough. He examined Yates and Chamberlain. Both men were dead.

Baxter punched the spent shells from his .44 and inserted fresh cartridges. Then he holstered the weapon and walked over to Olivera who was leaning with his back against the trunk of the pine. His hands were still bound behind his back, and the noose was still around his neck, but the pressure was gone from it.

Prison had not gone well with Olivera, Baxter thought. The man was gaunt. His cheeks were sunken, and his dark skin had a sickly tinge to it. There were streaks of gray in his black hair. Only the eyes burned with the same intensity of the old days.

Olivera stood there, legs spread a little, his chest rising and falling as he stared at Baxter. The hate was still in Olivera's eyes, but there seemed to be something else, something like puzzlement.

Baxter drew a deep breath. "I want you to listen to me, Olivera," he said. "I'm going to turn you loose, but first I want to tell you this. I know what you've got on your mind, and I don't blame you. The years haven't been pleasant for me, either, *amigo,* but I know they were nothing compared to what yours must have been."

He took out his knife and cut the thongs about Olivera's wrists, then stepped back. Olivera began to rub his wrists, his eyes all the while studying Baxter. Olivera did not speak for some time. Then he said: "Why do you do this?"

"I owe it to you."

"You know I have sworn to kill you?"

Baxter nodded.

"You saved my life," said Olivera, "and that puts me under an obligation to you, but there is still another life to be settled for. It is what I have broken out of prison for. It is the one thing that kept me alive, *hombre*. I swore an oath. In my María's blood I swore it. You have a gun, and I am unarmed. You had better kill me, Baxter."

"If a gun is what you want, you'll find one over there," said Baxter, indicating the bodies of Chamberlain and Yates.

Olivera peered at him a moment, hard, as though trying to see inside Baxter's brain. Then he strode over to Chamberlain's body. With the toe of his boot, Olivera rolled the man over. There was a six-shooter thrust into Chamberlain's waist. Olivera bent down and took the gun.

He straightened with the weapon in his hand. Baxter's .44 was still in its holster. Baxter's heart skipped a beat as he watched Olivera. The man stood there, fondling the gun, struggling with something in his mind. His teeth showed once in the beginning of a ferine snarl. Then, abruptly, he slipped the gun into the holster at his side.

"I have never killed a man in cold blood," said Olivera. "Not even for my María could I do it."

"Thank you, *amigo,*" said Baxter

"I have just given you your life like you gave me mine. We are even."

"Even," said Baxter.

"Bueno," said Olivera.

He went into a crouch. Baxter watched him with slitted eyes. This was the time for it, Baxter thought, this was what he had come into the Diablos for. He realized that there was a good chance he would die, but there was no regret in Baxter. This was the code he lived by.

He saw Olivera begin his draw. Baxter pulled his .44 with all the speed he possessed. He saw Olivera's gun whip up. The big bore gaped at him. He saw flame spurt out of it, but his .44 had already roared. Something whined past his head, and then Olivera was buckling.

The man went down to his knees. His head lifted, and he

started to bring his gun up again, but, when he had it level, it began to shake violently. Then it dropped from his fingers, unfired, and Olivera fell on his side.

He had rolled over on his back, when Baxter came up and knelt beside him. The blood was pumping out of the wound in Olivera's chest. His face held the color of death. He looked up at Baxter and smiled a little.

"You are the only real man I have ever known, *amigo,*" said Olivera. "Will you give me your hand before I die?"

Weakly Olivera lifted a hand, and Baxter took it. "Thank you, *amigo,*" he whispered, and died.

Mike McCall heard the shooting, and he rode by soon after that. He took one look at Baxter's face and decided against talking. Without a word, they lifted the bodies across the saddles of the mounts they had ridden. Only after this was done did the sheriff speak.

"You want to tell me anything, Dan?"

"I owed it to him," said Baxter. "It was the only thing that kept him alive in the pen. He did not care to live without his María. It was only a question of time before he died. I owed him a crack at me. He could have killed me, if he'd wanted to, but he was too much of a man for that."

McCall took another look at Baxter's face. "I think I understand," he said. He put an arm briefly on Baxter's shoulder. "Shall we go home?"

"Sure," said Baxter, thinking of Penny. He felt free. For the first time in five years he felt really free.

The Ways of Vengeance

The Z Bar D brand had been burned into a slab of wood nailed to the crossbar of the wide gate. Without dismounting, Nolan opened it, rode through, then carefully closed it. As he straightened in his saddle, he felt a sudden twinge in his thigh, and winced. It was not pain, however, but a flash of recollection that had made him flinch.

Six years, Wade, he thought, *six long years. There were times when I thought I'd never see this day. Have you ever thought that, too?*

He followed the road to where it crossed a small plank bridge across a wash. A trickle of water in the bottom of the arroyo was a reminder of the flood waters that raged through this gash in the earth after heavy rains on the mountain. His black's hoofs rang hollowly on the boards. In the willows on the other side of the bridge Nolan reined the black horse in.

For a while he studied the ranch buildings ahead, eyes crinkling with concentration, the unshaven planes of his cheeks gaunt and grim. All he spied was one person moving about, and that man certainly was not Wade Dunmire, unless Wade had changed radically. This fellow moved too slowly, and there was a hitch to his stride. Nolan's thigh twinged again, and he cursed softly.

It'll be over before long now, he comforted himself. *Six years of waiting and hunting will soon be over.* He touched the black lightly with the spurs.

The man near the ranch house spotted Nolan riding in

and stood there, waiting, his left leg thrust out a little, awkwardly and stiffly. He was an old man whose white whiskers stirred in the breeze off the mountain.

Nolan reined in. There was no hostility in the old man's eyes but no friendliness, either — only a calm passivity that said he would wait before speaking until Nolan explained himself.

Nolan glanced about, eyes quick and searching. There was no one here save the old man.

"Dunmire around?" Nolan asked.

The old man shook his head.

"Where is he?"

The old man's blue eyes brightened. They studied Nolan, taking in the dust on his clothing, the bleak, gaunt look of his face, the hang of the black-handled pistol at his leg.

"He won't be home until nightfall." The old man's voice was as soft and tired as a breeze, sighing in the tops of pines.

"I'll wait," Nolan said, and stepped down from the black.

"It's a long time until nightfall," the old man said.

"I'll wait, anyway."

Nolan led the black over to the water tank beside the windmill. While the horse drank, Nolan thought — *a long time until nightfall?* The smile that touched his lips held no mirth. *What's a few hours measured against six years?*

He sat down in the shade on the front steps, watching the old man move about the yard. He moved slowly and painfully, dragging his left leg. Obviously, the knee was quite stiff. He glanced now and then at Nolan but made no attempt to speak.

Nolan studied the buildings. There was this house, a bunkshack, a shed, and corrals. The set-up did not look too prosperous, but the buildings were in good repair. The lack of prosperity did not surprise Nolan. This had been a hard year for men who ran cattle.

For the first time in six years he thought of something else than the vengeance which had at last brought him here. When this day was over, then what? Cattle was all he knew. He supposed he would go back to that business, catching on wherever he could. Maybe someday he'd have his own spread. But there was little joy in this line of thinking.

June, he thought, and for an instant he felt like weeping. *June.*

He was snapped out of this reverie by the sound of the door opening behind his back. He straightened and rolled around on one hip, his hand jerking the pistol halfway out of the holster before he saw who it was.

The little girl who stood there, a trifle startled, was hugging a doll to her breast, and her eyes were wide as she stared at him. She was no more than five, and the sight of her brought unexpected shame and confusion. He could feel the hot blood warm his face as he shoved the pistol back in holster.

"Who are you?" There was a growl in his voice, even though he did not mean it to be there.

"Kathy," the child said.

"Kathy who?"

"Kathy Dunmire. Who are you?"

"Is there anybody else here?"

"Sure. Uncle Josh."

Nolan pointed at the old man who was forking hay in a corral. "Is that him?"

"Uhn-huh."

"Where's your mother?"

The little girl did not answer, only watched him solemnly, the doll's head pressed against her cheek.

"Is she inside?" Nolan asked.

"No."

"Where is she?"

"She's gone away."

"When will she be back?"

"I don't know. She's gone far away. My daddy says I'll see her some day, but I have to wait. I don't cry any more. I used to once, when I was little. What's your name? You haven't told me."

He looked away, toward the mountain and beyond it, far beyond it. He knew what loss was. After a while he said: "Is anyone else here?"

"Sure."

"Who?"

"Zoe."

"Zoe? Who is she?"

"My dolly. She's all I've got to play with. Uncle Josh plays with me sometimes, but he's not much fun. Daddy is always too tired to play. He works hard." She stared at him gravely. "Why are you mad at me?"

"I'm not mad at you."

"Then why do you look at me like that?"

It dawned on him that he had been staring at her rather hard. *Yes, why?* he asked himself. Was it the old yearning that had never been satisfied? The pain, he suddenly realized, had never been quite as deep and sharp as it was right now. He rose to his feet.

"Aren't you going to tell me your name?" she asked again.

"Dave," he said, and headed for the corrals, eyes seeking the old man. But after a moment they shifted past the old fellow into the vast distances beyond the mountain and the sky.

Kathy's Uncle Josh had finished feeding the horses penned in the corrals. He made sure the gate was shut securely, then turned and waited for Nolan to come up. The burdens of the years drooped old Josh's shoulders, but his eyes were bright and searching as they watched Dave Nolan.

"About Dunmire," Nolan said. "Where is he? In town?"

Josh paused before replying. He jerked his head at the mountain. "He's up there, fixing a drift fence." Another pause. "We've been losing too many strays."

Strays, Nolan thought, and anger flared in him, old and vicious and all-consuming. Then he got himself in hand, again soothing himself. *It'll soon be over. It'll be over, and then I can begin to forget.*

He averted his glance because the old man's eyes, wise from experience, seemed to be reading what lay behind his own. As he asked — "He up there alone?" — he could hear the quickened beating of his heart.

Josh nodded.

"You the only hired hand?"

A sad, bitter smile touched Josh's lips. "If you want to call me that." He stared down at his left leg. "He can't afford anyone else. Times are hard. I do some chores and look after the girl while he's away." His head came up. His eyes sharpened, as did his tone. "Just what you want with Dunmire?"

"It'll keep until I see him," Nolan said.

"He's not hiring. You might try the Drag A up the valley. I don't think it would do you any good, but you could try. They're the biggest outfit in these parts."

"I'm not looking for work."

"What are you looking for, then?"

Nolan caught the quick, discerning glance the old man

threw at the pistol, but it did not bother Dave. *Let him look,* he thought. *I don't care what he figures out. Only one thing matters and that's not far off, not more than a few hours.*

"I have business with him," Nolan said.

"Personal?"

"Personal."

The old man's eyes grew sad. They mirrored the futility he must feel with death so near at hand for him. He seemed to be asking: why rush it, when it came too soon anyway?

"He won't be back until dark," Josh said.

"I'll wait," Nolan said again.

The sadness deepened in the old man's eyes. He sighed. "Yes," he murmured. "I guess you will."

He started off, dragging his left foot. The sight made Nolan remember the twinges that came every now and then to his own leg. He thought there had just been another one, but he wasn't sure. The only thing of which he could be sure was the melancholy and the anguish in his heart.

At first he was so caught up in the remembrance of grief that he forgot the thing. Now it came to him, suddenly. The knowing look in Josh's eyes, and something else. Something like — the glint of steel?

He crossed the yard with long strides and was in the bunkshack almost on Josh's heels. The old man heard him coming and moaned a little as he tore the Winchester from the pegs on the wall.

He tried to move fast, but the years and the stiffness in his knee foiled him. His mouth opened, strained with pain. He emitted a short, sharp gasp as he tried to cock the rifle and throw down on Nolan.

Nolan had youth and the drive of hate on his side. He closed in swiftly, before Josh could set himself. Nolan's left hand smashed the rifle barrel aside and up. Then he grabbed it with his right hand also and, with a violent jerk, tore it out of Josh's grasp. The old man lurched forward, but then a spasm of pain stole the last of his strength, and he slammed up against the wall.

He stood there, bracing himself on wide-spread legs, the good one and the bad one, and sobbed.

"You son- . . . ," he swore. "You dirty son-of-a-bitch, you!"

Anger and effort had Nolan breathing hard. "I don't like to do this," he said, "but I'm not letting anyone spoil things for me, not when I've waited this long."

When Josh lay in his bunk, bound hand and foot, Nolan glared down at him. "Whether or not I gag you, depends on you. Just start hollering, and I'll shut you up."

The old man was quiet. Tiredness lay deeper than ever in his features. His eyes reflected the misery he felt over his failure, but mixed in with this was a sharp glimmer of hate. Nolan felt this on his back all the way across the threshold.

He sat on the steps of the house again and watched the little girl at play. She had a couple of boxes, and on one of these she propped the doll. The doll, however, kept toppling over, and, every time the girl righted the doll, she scolded it severely.

He sat and listened to the childish prattle from a world of dreams and fancies. It made him remember his own childhood, how happy and free from anxieties and heartbreak it had been. It was a pity, he thought, that anyone had to grow up. The world was too cruel and sad a place.

The little girl was a blonde. Seeing the sun glisten in her hair made him remember. Golden blonde, he had called it, the yellow gold of ripening wheat. He could almost see it now.

* * * * *

He had no idea how *she* had got there. But he could see her coming toward him. She was so far away he could not make out her features, but the sun rioting in her yellow hair told him who she was. He rose to his feet, trembling with excitement and dread.

He tried to call her name, but his throat was suddenly dry, and the walls constricted so that he could not manage the slightest sound. He could only stand and watch her come, with hunger and longing crying in his heart.

When he finally could make out her face, the first thing he noticed were the tears. This was something he could not understand. There should be no tears. Why should there be when they were together?

He reached a hand out to her, and she stopped and glared at him with the tears, trickling down her cheeks. He tried to move toward her, but his legs would not stir. Her mouth worked. She seemed to be trying to tell him something, but the words were strangely garbled, so that he could not understand. Then she turned and started to walk away.

His legs functioned now. He started after her with long strides, but as fast as he moved, she moved faster. He could see her receding into the far distances with such rapidity he knew he could never overtake her.

"June!" he shouted at the top of his voice. "June!"

"What's the matter, Dave?"

He blinked his eyes to clear them of the sleep that had so suddenly come over him. Only now did he realize how tired he was. He stared at the little girl who stood in front of him, watching him solemnly.

"Why did you holler?"

He passed a hand over his face, pressing the fingers

against his aching eyes. Anguish whimpered in him a moment, then was gone.

"I just had a dream," he said. "That's all."

"I dream, too. Sometimes I get scared and I holler, and then Daddy comes and wakes me up. Were you scared, Dave?"

He stared off beyond the mountain. "No. Not exactly."

"Why did you holler, then?"

"I . . . I don't know."

"Zoe dreams, too," Kathy said, hugging the doll closer, "and she hollers, too. When she does that, I just pick her up and rock her and sing to her until she goes back to sleep. Do you want me to sing to you?"

He looked at her. The small face was grave and earnest. The wide eyes watched him solicitously. He felt something wrench at his heart and then anger came again.

If you think this is going to stop me, Wade, he thought, *you've got another think coming. It didn't stop you, did it?*

"Don't you want me to sing, Dave?"

"Some other time."

"How long are you going to stay?"

"Until . . . ," he began, then caught himself. "Not for long."

"Are you waiting for Daddy?"

"Yes."

"He won't be home until it's dark. He told me that, when he left this morning. Where's Uncle Josh?"

He could not help a quick glance at the bunkshack. He looked at the girl, but she did not understand.

"He's . . . gone," he said. "To do some chores. I think he said there's some new calves he has to look after. He'll be back soon."

"He didn't take me," she pouted. "He always does. Once

there was a baby calf and her mama died and Uncle Josh fed her with a bottle." She giggled. "It was cute. I liked to watch that." Then she pouted again. "But he didn't take me this time. He never leaves me alone. Will you stay with me until he comes back?"

Something filled his throat, and he had to clear it before he could speak. Somehow this angered him. "I'll stay," he said. "Don't worry."

She smiled. "I'm not scared any more, then. I'm not scared with you around."

He stared down at the ground. *Kathy,* he thought, *when you're grown up, I wonder if . . . ? You're going to have to learn early, Kathy. You're going to have to learn early how cruel the world really is.*

Josh lay trussed in his bunk and stared at Nolan with hate. This meant nothing to Nolan. Long ago, he had put everything aside, hopes and dreams and ambitions, because these had no place in his life until the job he had set for himself was done. Other people's feelings toward him, whether good or bad, bothered him not at all.

He checked the ropes that bound the old man, then stepped back. The old eyes, wise and knowing and helpless now, never left him.

"What have you got against Dunmire?" Josh asked.

Nolan's lips felt stiff, as though they had not been used in a long time. "A matter of business . . . old business."

"You mean to kill him, don't you?"

Nolan made no answer. His eyes shifted, to the vast distances that held so many memories.

"Why?" the old man asked. "Dunmire's a good man. He came to this valley five years ago and has never been in any trouble. He's well liked."

Nolan smiled faintly, without humor. He said nothing.

"He's had his share of bad luck," Josh said. A plea had entered his voice. "First his wife. Then hard times. Is what you've got against him bad enough that you've got to kick a man when he's down?"

Nolan turned on the old man with a fury that blanched Josh. "Nothing I could ever do to him would be bad enough for him. What I really should. . . ." He caught himself then. His teeth clenched, and the muscles bulged along his jaw. Abruptly he wheeled and went out, shutting the bunkhouse door behind him.

He had unsaddled the black and tied the mount to a cottonwood in the shade. Now he carried a forkful of hay over to the horse. He talked to the animal a while and patted the sleek neck. Then he returned to the house.

Kathy was standing on the bottom step, hanging onto the doll with one arm while with her other hand she grubbed at her eyes. Grime made a ring around her mouth, and there were streaks of dirt on her bare arms.

"I'm hungry," she complained.

He looked at her in irritation. "Don't you have anything to eat in the house?"

"Sure. But Uncle Josh always fixes it for me. Where is he, Dave?"

He couldn't meet her eyes. "I told you he went to look after some calves. He'll be back soon."

"I'm hungry."

"Well, go inside and eat."

"I don't know how to cook. I can't start the fire."

"All right, all right. Come on, I'll see what I can do."

He found some fatback and beans and fixed these. He also made some coffee. She sat on a chair and followed his every move with big eyes. When he poured the coffee, she said: "I always drink milk. Daddy wants me to."

"I don't see any milk around."

She giggled. "Silly. You've got to milk a cow first. Don't you know that? That's what Uncle Josh does."

He could not understand what it was in him, whether anger or embarrassment or confusion. "Well, I'm not milking any cow. If you don't want coffee, drink water."

While she ate, he sat and watched her. Somehow he could not take his eyes off her golden hair. It made him think and wonder.

If ours had been born, he thought, *would it have had yellow hair, if it had been a girl? You were a blonde, June, your hair like wheat ripe in the field. Maybe she'd have been a blonde, too. I think I would have liked that. I think I. . . .* A sudden welling of grief made him bow his head and pass his hand over his face.

"What's the matter, Dave?"

He lifted his head. The grim purpose still lived in him, stronger than ever now.

"Don't you feel good?"

"Eat your dinner," he growled.

"I'm full. I can't eat another bite."

Nolan gathered the dirty dishes and put them in a large pan. While he was doing this, he felt something touch his leg. Glancing down, he saw her tugging at his trousers, just below the tip of his holster. The small face was clear, free from guile.

"I like you," she said with childish simplicity and directness.

He averted his eyes. *Did she know? With a child's wisdom had she guessed what lay in his mind? It makes no difference,* he thought. *I've waited too long. I've suffered too much. You'll suffer, too, Kathy, but that's the way life is. It's just your tough luck that you've got to learn sooner than most. . . .*

Josh blinked his eyes in surprise, when he saw the tin plate filled with fatback and beans. Nolan freed the old man's hands, then pulled his bound legs over the edge of the bunk, so that Josh could sit up. Josh needed no urging. He ate without Nolan's having to say a word.

When the old man was through, Nolan bound his arms again. Josh watched Nolan unblinkingly now, a new and sad understanding in his blue eyes.

"Have you ever killed a man, Nolan?" Josh asked.

"No."

"But you are going to kill Dunmire?"

"That's right."

"It's not like you, Nolan. A man like you can't hate that much."

"Can't I?" Suddenly it was there in Nolan, the compulsion to tell everything. All these years he had kept it to himself, torturing himself with memories, never seeking surcease. Now it came tumbling out of him. He could not have stopped the words, if he had tried.

"Do you want to know why?" he asked, turning on Josh. His voice was low, hoarse. "It was in Texas, on the open range. Cattle stray fifty miles, a hundred miles. You round up the strays, brand the calves, return the cattle to the owners, and they pay you a dollar a head. That was my business . . . and Dunmire's."

He paused to draw a breath. Talking about it had started something crying inside him, something plaintive and lost. He went on. "It doesn't matter what there was between us. We were rivals, and we did things to each other, me as much as him. We quarreled over who was to work which territory.

I had my wife with me. I didn't want her there, but she wanted to help."

He paused again. His thigh twinged as though in echo — or was it mockery? "Anyway, Dunmire stampeded some cattle through my camp. June . . . my wife . . . couldn't move fast. I tried to get to her, but I was thrown, and my leg got busted. When the stampede had passed and I crawled to her, there was nothing left . . . either of her, or of the child we would have had."

He came out of it — how much later he never knew — to find the old man watching him. When Nolan looked at him, old Josh glanced away.

"I'm sorry, Nolan," old Josh said.

"That doesn't help any."

Through the window he saw that the sun was going down. With an effort he put grief aside. He rummaged around in Josh's warbag until he found a bandanna.

"I'm going to have to gag you now," he said. "I won't have you hollering out to warn him."

Kathy had the doll sitting on one of the steps and was scolding her because she had been disobedient. The setting sun glistened where it struck the golden hair. Nolan slitted his eyes and clenched his teeth.

"Come with me, Kathy," he said.

She looked up with a happy smile. "Where?"

"In the house."

The smile died. "I thought we were going somewhere. Maybe to get Uncle Josh. A horseback ride?" The smile returned.

Dave Nolan had never felt this grim. He supposed it was because the time was at hand. "No. We're just going in the house."

"Why?"

Annoyance and impatience — was there also something else? — hardened his tone. "Because I said so."

He saw the bewildered look on the little face as he took her hand. For the first time a flicker of fear crossed the tiny features, but at the touch of his fingers it vanished. She went with him without another word.

He took her to the bedroom. When he released her hand, she turned and looked up at him, openly puzzled. Somehow he was reluctant to leave, even though the time was growing urgent. He put his hand momentarily on her head.

"Kathy . . . ," he said. It was difficult for him to speak. "I'm going to have to shut you in here."

"Why?"

"I can't tell you."

The small lower lip came out and trembled. "Have I been naughty?"

"No, Kathy, you've been very good."

"Then why are you punishing me?"

"I'm not punishing you. I . . . there's nothing else I can do."

"I promise to be good, Dave."

He could feel it getting him and that wouldn't do at all. He couldn't weaken now, not after six years of waiting. "Maybe some day you'll understand," he said gruffly. "If you never do. . . ."

Abruptly he turned and left, bolting the door behind him. Before he had gone two steps, she began to cry.

He saddled the black and left it ground-hitched behind the house. After that, he took up a post just around a corner of the building. He checked the pistol once, but it was ready, as it had been for six years.

The little girl was still crying. Puzzled and frightened, she sobbed in the room, and he could hear her, faintly. The sound touched his heart but not all the way. Nothing could ever reach deeply enough to get past the hate and grim resolution.

The sun was down. Shadows were thickening throughout the valley. The mountain became shrouded in darkness.

The sound of crying continued, but now it seemed as though another voice had joined the little girl's, another voice he knew well. *June?*

Something frigid touched the back of his neck, and he shivered. He remembered suddenly all the times he had dreamed of her and how she had always cried in those dreams, and how he had always had the idea she was trying to tell him something.

What, June? he thought. *What do you want me to know, to understand?*

From out of the dusk came a sound. Nolan tensed, listening hard. Had it been the far-off ring of a shod hoof against stone? One of the horses in the corrals nickered, and from out in the night a whinny answered.

Nolan drew his pistol, then froze as comprehension dawned.

He crouched there, tight against the wall of the house, pistol clutched in a sweating palm, listening to the sounds of a horse coming in. Then the voice, the well-remembered, well-hated voice.

"Josh? Where are you, Josh?"

He should have put a light in the bunkshack and one in the house, Nolan thought. They would have made things look natural and unsuspicious. But it didn't matter any more, not with what he understood now.

"Josh?" Dunmire called anxiously. "What the hell, Josh? Kathy?"

Nolan saw the dark hulk of the man, sitting his horse in

front of the bunkshack. An easy shot. A sure shot. Nolan turned and left. The black shied as he gathered up the reins, stepped up into saddle, and rode quietly away.

He had a glimpse once of a little girl, lost in a child's world, a world that should never end, but always did. He had a glimpse of a little girl who, from now on when he dreamed of his June, would no longer be crying. *For you and her, Kathy,* he thought, *for the two of you. It's what she would want.*

The black moved on, hoofs clopping softly in the night. When they topped the rim, a gust of wind struck Nolan. It felt fresh and clean.

Fear in the Saddle

Travis awoke and lay a while, listening to the sounds coming from the corral. In his mind's eye he could see the restless pacing of the roan. It seemed that the animal was never still. In one way this might be a good thing, for this constant fitfulness could tire the animal, thus making the job ahead a trifle easier. But just thinking about it turned Travis cold at the pit of his stomach.

Travis rose and dressed. He cursed a little, quietly and disgustedly, while he cooked his breakfast. He wondered if he could get anything down. He kept thinking about what he had to do this morning.

Down in the corral the roan still paced.

Although there was no taste to it, Travis forced some food into himself. Then he built a cigarette and sat with his legs stretched out to savor an after-breakfast smoke. He told himself there was nothing better than a cigarette after eating, but he knew the real reason was that it helped prolong the time before he went to the roan.

Finally, he rose to his feet, full of disgust with himself. After all, this wasn't the first time he'd tried to break a horse! He'd been doing this for ten of his twenty-five years. This was his livelihood. He'd ridden the buckers in Calgary, Pendleton, Cheyenne. He was one of the best riders in the business. He'd topped tougher bronchos than this wild roan that he'd captured a month ago. But all that lay in the past, he realized sickeningly. This was something different.

He decided it was no good, standing here, thinking about

it. The thoughts only tormented him. The thing to do was to get it over with.

The roan heard Travis coming and abruptly stopped his pacing. He turned to face Travis, ears cocked, tense and waiting. The roan snorted once, then was quiet, watching Travis crossing to the corral.

Travis stopped and stared through the bars, and, as he looked, he thought he felt a pain in his right thigh where his leg had been broken. But that had happened over a year ago, and more than one doctor had pronounced the leg healed. Still, the pain persisted as Travis stood there. He knew it was only in his mind, but it felt real enough. He began to sweat.

Travis clenched his teeth and stepped into the corral. The roan snorted and paced nervously to the far end of the enclosure.

Travis shook out a loop in his rope. He didn't have too much trouble with the roan. By now the animal had grown accustomed to being roped and snubbed and saddled. Travis had been patient with the horse. He had taught him first to become used to a halter, then to a blanket on his back, then the saddle, and finally weights on the saddle.

Now it was time to ride the roan. Travis felt weak and sick.

The horse was snubbed tightly to a post which Travis had sunk into the ground at one end of the corral. He stood docilely enough, tension apparent only in the way he flicked back his ears.

Travis stood undecided. He told himself he couldn't be too careful. This abandoned ranch he had selected for his job was in an isolated part of these mountains. No one ever passed by here. A man could not be too careful with a wild horse, when he was by himself. But Travis had to be alone.

The shame was so great in him he could not endure the thought of displaying his cowardice to another.

Travis began to feel that he should try a weight on the roan again today. Perhaps the horse wasn't ready to be ridden yet. He had to be careful about that because he was alone, Travis thought, and then he flushed with disgust and mortification. He knew this was just another excuse to put off riding the roan.

Travis could feel the muscles of his thighs quivering as he quietly loosened the rope, holding the roan snubbed. For a wild instant he hoped the roan would jerk away from him so he couldn't mount, but the animal stood quietly, not flicking a muscle.

Travis sucked in his breath, and then he was going up into the saddle. The roan reacted swiftly. Even before Travis touched the seat of the kak, the animal was going up in the air, his back arching. Travis's boots found the stirrups quickly.

The roan kept his back arched and began crow-hopping across the corral. This maneuver would never have been enough to unseat Travis in the past. But he envisioned himself being hurtled through the air and then striking the ground and the roan bearing down on him, forehoofs rising, flailing, to come crashing down on him as he cowered helplessly on the ground.

He was alone, his mind shrieked at him. He had to unload of his own will. He had to pile off of his own choosing, if he didn't want to be trampled again. There was no one around to drive off the roan and drag him away as there had been in Calgary. Panic filled Travis's throat.

He hit the ground on both feet, and the momentum of it carried him forward and down, but he spread his hands before him and saved himself from going flat on his face.

You've got to get out of here! You've got to run before he tramples you!

Then he was on his feet and streaking for the corral bars. Terror shrieked in his brain. He went through the bars so fast he sprawled on the ground, his cheek scraping the dirt. For a moment he lay there, breathing hard, quivering, and sick with fear, afraid to rise and afraid almost to hope that he was safe. But the worst of the panic soon passed, and Travis rolled over and sat up.

He stared at the corral and saw the roan on the far side, watching him. It came then to Travis that the horse had made no effort to trample him. The instant he had quit the saddle, the roan must have stopped bucking. The horse wasn't even breathing hard. He stood there with ears cocked forward, looking at Travis, as if he understood what had gone on in the man's mind.

Travis put his face in his hands and shuddered. He could have wept with helplessness.

He lay on his bunk, blowing cigarette smoke up at the ceiling. The quivering of his insides had stopped, and fear seemed a distant and alien thing to him now. He supposed it was because he had knocked off for the rest of the day and wouldn't have to face the job until the next morning.

He told himself there was no compulsion about this thing except what he himself wanted to do. It wasn't necessary for him to follow the rodeo circuit to earn his keep. He could do all right in some other line of business. It wasn't even a question of being unable to ride a horse. The broken ones he could ride without a qualm. It was the buckers that turned him hollow and quivering inside, but he didn't have to stick to broncho-riding for a living.

I guess I'll quit, he thought, puffing slowly on his smoke.

It wouldn't be too hard to give a reason. I can say I'm all busted up inside, and the docs have told me never to top a bronc' again.

But he felt ill and miserable at the thought. Whatever he might tell others, he himself would know he had quit because he was afraid. He was yellow.

Travis turned his face to the wall and cursed with a studied, frustrated vehemence. *Yellow,* his mind kept whispering. He just didn't have any guts any more.

Travis awoke before dawn. He lay a while in his bunk, listening for sounds from the corral, but they didn't begin until the break of day. Then, because he couldn't stand hearing them and because he wanted to get an early start, Travis jumped out of bed.

After breakfast, he went outside. The morning was clear and cool. There was a stiff breeze coming down from the mountain, stirring the tops of the pines and cedars, and raising occasional, small swirls of dust in the corral. The roan was staring almost wistfully out through the bars, at the timbered slopes and pitches. He seemed immersed in this study and paid no attention to Travis as he came down from the house.

Travis stopped and watched the roan a while. The horse still did not face Travis, although he must have heard the jingle of his spurs as Travis had come up. He just went on staring, with a longing that was apparent to the man.

Travis found himself thinking: *It's a shame to coop him up like this. He never hurt anybody. He wants to be out there, free and wild. He should be turned loose.*

Then the feeling came that this was just the old excuse taking another turn. It was the cowardice working in him.

Angry with himself, he stepped into the corral. He roped the roan and snubbed him to the post. The horse was quite difficult this morning, and there was a fine film of sweat on Travis's face by the time he got the animal tied to the post. The roan wouldn't stand still. He knocked the saddle off three times, before Travis got it cinched on.

"I don't like this any more than you do," he growled at the horse, "but it's something that has to be done. If you'd just go along with me, we'd get it over with that much faster. Now stand still, or I'll take a whip to you."

The instant that Travis released the snub, the roan jerked away. Travis grabbed for the lines, but the roan moved so fast and hard that the reins were ripped out of Travis's grip. Snorting, the roan whirled and raced to the other end of the corral.

Cursing savagely, Travis went after the roan, but, before he was within ten feet of the animal, the roan broke wildly past him, spraying him with grit and dust kicked up by his pounding hoofs. Travis got his rope. He shook out a loop and advanced on the roan. For an instant the horse bared his teeth, and his ears flattened against his head. The roan emitted a shrill, angry snort and broke.

The horse seemed to hurtle straight at Travis, and he had a swift, terrifying vision of going down under those churning hoofs, but at the last instant the roan swerved, and, as he pounded past him, Travis dropped the loop over his neck. The roan fought all the way back to the snubbing-post, but Travis finally got him tied again.

Travis was breathing hard. The roan kept shying and snorting, and Travis saw it was no use trying to do anything with the horse until the roan had calmed down. He was angry again, at himself and at the horse. If things had not gone wrong, he might have had the ordeal over with by this time, he might have had the roan broken by now. Instead, he still had to start, and, as he waited, watching the roan, he could feel the first tentative flutters of fear in his thighs and in his belly. He knew that in a little while he was going to feel sick again, and he almost wept with anger.

He edged in on the roan and caught the halter and began patting the horse's neck. "I'm not going to hurt you, boy," he told the roan. "It's just something that's got to be done. For myself. Damn it, why do you keep fighting me?"

The roan quieted. The wicked, perverse glint seemed to go out of his eyes. Now he stood there, almost still.

"We're going to get along all right together. I know we are," Travis said, with an assurance he didn't feel. He kept stroking the roan's neck.

The roan was very still now. He seemed relaxed and no longer vigilant. Continuing to stroke him with his right hand, Travis released the snap with his left, and, before the roan realized that once more he was free, Travis had vaulted up into the saddle.

The roan whirled around twice as he pulled away from the post. Travis had both feet in the stirrups, and this time he had a good seat, and for a moment he was almost overwhelmed with confidence.

Travis could feel his body sway with the old ease and effortlessness with the first harsh movements of the roan, and he almost sang with joy. The roan kicked up his hind end and then reared sharply. Then he started whirling again, raising a great cloud of dust that almost gagged Travis, but Travis went along with it, sticking like a burr to the saddle, exulting all the while.

Abruptly the roan changed tactics. His back arched, and he began hopping stiff-legged across the corral. With each try the horse seemed to go higher and come down harder. The jolts began to jar up Travis's spine. He felt the joy, the assurance, ebb from him.

It was not a question of sticking in the saddle any more, he thought. He was sure he could do that, but there was something wrong inside him. His belly was filled with pain. It was as if the jolts had torn something loose in there, and it kept bouncing up and down, agonizingly, with each movement of the roan.

The doctors had lied. He wasn't cured at all. He was all torn up and busted inside. He could feel something break loose and rise up to gag in his throat. He couldn't breathe. He was a sick man. He had no business on a bucking horse.

The roan had reached the other end of the corral, and now he swerved up against the poles, trying to scrape Travis off the saddle. Travis saw the bars come at him, and he waited for no more. He threw himself wildly out of the kak. He hit the ground and went sprawling. But he recovered quickly and was halfway to his feet when the roan hit him.

It was so sudden and unexpected that, at first, Travis had no idea he had been struck. He felt himself being barreled along over the ground, and only then it occurred to him that the roan had turned on him.

Panic clogged Travis's throat. Luckily, he had been knocked toward the side of the corral, and, as the roan, squealing with rage, came smashing back, Travis rolled to safety beneath the bottom bar.

He lurched up on his knees, trembling with fear and fury. His face was wet, but he didn't know if it was from sweat or tears or blood. His thigh ached furiously, and for a moment he was afraid that his leg had been broken again.

The roan smashed up against the side of the corral once more. Then the horse put his head down between his front legs and went bucking frenziedly around the enclosure. Travis shook his fist at the roan.

"I'll fix you," he shouted. "I'll show you, if you can get away with this!"

He jumped to his feet, raging with defeat and frustration, and ran up to the house. He got his Winchester and ran back to the corral.

"Damn you," he screamed at the roan, "see how you like this!"

He had the sights lined up with the roan's head, when a sudden thought struck him, and he froze.

He was all right inside. There was nothing wrong with his belly, there was nothing loose in him, there was nothing clogging his throat any more. It had been panic that had caused the pain and had thrown him off the roan.

You're really yellow, Travis, an inner voice said to him.

"I'm not yellow," he said aloud. "It's that damn' devil in there. He scraped me off. I'm not yellow." He was almost sobbing. The rifle fell from his shoulder. "How can I be yellow, all the tough bronc's I've topped?"

The misery and shame combined with the rage that remained in him still. "Damn you," he cried at the roan, and began to slide between the poles into the corral. "I'll show you, if I'm yellow. You scrape me off again, and I'll put a slug through your brain!"

He ran up to the roan in a frenzy and made a grab for the reins, but the horse whirled and galloped away. Half blind with fury, panting, cursing, sobbing, Travis snatched his rope and went after the roan. He cornered him and dropped the loop over his neck, and then, hand over hand, he went swiftly up to the lunging, plunging animal.

The roan started to rear, but Travis had a good hold on the hackamore, and he wouldn't let go. The roan snorted and swung away, but Travis, raging, hung on. He made a wild, leaping grab for the saddle horn and caught it and went up into the saddle.

The roan, squealing with fury, was pitching and lunging even before Travis hit the kak. The jolt of it cracked his teeth together, but he stayed on and caught up the lines and found the flapping stirrups with his boots.

The roan was in the full grip of his fury as he went bucking savagely across the corral. Travis didn't expect to stay on. He hadn't guessed that the roan could be so savage. Those other attempts had been picnics compared to this try. He expected to be thrown momentarily.

Realizing that defeat was imminent, the rage in Travis grew. As the jolts jarred him, he began to scream: "Go on, pitch me off. Throw me, damn you! Throw me, and I'll put a slug in your brain!"

He was sobbing with anger. Stinging tears ran down his cheeks. He thought it might be blood, but he knew better. It was only his cowardice that made him think it was blood running out of his nose and mouth.

"Pitch me off," he screamed at the roan. "Throw me!"

The roan aimed for the side of the corral, but Travis saw it coming, and he swung his leg out of the way and stayed on the roan with only one foot in a stirrup to support him. The horse smashed with insane fury against the poles and rebounded, and Travis settled back in the kak again. His spurs raked the roan's flanks.

"Throw me," he shouted, knowing he didn't have long to go. "Pitch me off, you red devil. You'll throw me just once more. I promise you that!"

The wetness on his face tasted like blood, but he knew it was just his cowardice, playing tricks on him. He knew he would never conquer this fear. Once he went off the roan, he would never mount another bucker. Travis was sobbing openly now.

"What you waiting for? Damn it, come on and throw me!"

The roan squealed and reared high and for a breath-taking instant trembled there, then he came crashing down on his own back. But Travis had kicked free of the stirrups and was down on the ground as the roan crashed on his back. It was instinct more than anything else that sent Travis back into the saddle as the roan righted himself and lunged up on his feet. He started to rear again, and Travis raked hard with the spurs and sawed on the lines, and this time the roan did not crash over backward. He came down on his four hoofs and started crow-hopping.

"Throw me," Travis croaked. "Pitch me off, you devil. Throw me."

Finally it dawned on Travis that the jolts were not so hard any more. The roan's fury seemed to have diminished. His stiff-legged hopping was half-hearted, but Travis couldn't believe that he had triumphed.

The roan tried two more desultory hops and then brought up still, legs spraddled, foam-flecked flanks heaving. Travis could hear the whistling of the roan's breath, and he lifted a hand to wipe the sweat off his face, and he saw it was really blood that was running out of his nose.

Travis awoke and saw that it was evening. He rose, fully clothed, from his bunk and went outside. He was still sore from the effects of his ride, but it was a good stiffness. For the first time in more than a year he felt at peace with himself.

He walked slowly down to the corral. The roan was

standing listless, as if he, too, were fully spent. Travis stood and stared at the roan, and he began to feel something inside that he couldn't put into words. He guessed it was gratitude, and then he started to think it was more than that.

The roan turned his head once and looked at Travis. Then he dropped his head and just stood there. He no longer was a proud, untamed animal. His spirit was broken. The roan would make a good mount, Travis thought, but his fight was gone forever.

Travis wondered, then, if it had really been worth it.

The Return of the Arapaho Kid

He waited until the stagecoach had topped a rise and was gone from sight, with only its dust hanging yellow and shimmering in the desert air, and then he rode in with his sorrel picking its way through the sage and mesquite. I watched him come up. He hadn't done anything to me — not yet — but still I hated him for the memories he awakened and the ashes he had fanned into flame again.

He reined in the sorrel and sat in the saddle a while, watching me with a slight, crooked smile on his lean, bearded face. Then his eyes drifted past me and beyond the long, low stage station to where the grave was, its dirt heaped in a little mound and its wooden marker still fresh and not yet pitted by pelting grit and driving wind, and the small box of wilting flowers that Roslyn had placed there only this morning.

After a time his glance wandered back to me. "You don't seem at all glad to see me, Hardin," he said.

"That's right."

He shifted his seat, and saddle leather creaked. He swept the desert all around with a quick, searching look, but only the burning hills were there, and the purple-misted peaks of the Doloritas in the distance. The emptiness seemed to please him, and he slumped at ease in the saddle.

"I've got some talk to make with you," he said.

"There's nothing for us to talk about, McCall."

"But, my friend, there is . . . there is," he said, and showed me that sly, crooked grin again.

I heard the door behind me open, and the tapping on the floor of the gallery, and then the voice. "Quincey? Is that you, son?"

"No, Dad," I said gently. "It's not Quincey. Quincey's. . . ." I didn't finish.

Although I hadn't turned around, I could picture him standing there, hunched over his cane, his right side and arm and leg all but useless, and the left side of his face screwed up in the frozen squint that was the mark of the stroke he'd had. I could picture him peering hard with his pale blue eyes while his confused brain tried to understand.

"That's right," he said, and I knew that for a moment his mind was clear. "Quincey's dead. I keep forgetting."

I heard Roslyn then: "Come inside, Dad."

"But I want to sit out here, in the shade."

"Come, Dad." She had seen McCall. She hated him almost more than I did. The memories he awoke in her would be far sharper and more aching than mine. "You've got to finish your dinner."

"But I only want to sit here a minute, Roslyn," I heard him complain. But he went in, nevertheless. His cane made small, lonely sounds.

"You can water your horse," I told McCall, "and then get."

"Now wait a minute, my friend," he said, holding up a protesting hand. His mouth was crooked. "Aren't you forgetting him?" he asked, nodding to where Dad had gone inside. "You want me to tell him about Quincey and the Arapaho Kid?"

We sat in the shade of the barn by the corrals. The horses that had pulled the stage from Encinal still showed the marks of the harness on their sweating hides. They stood quietly, eating their hay and switching their tails at the flies. They would be well rested by the time the stage made the return trip from Silver Hill.

"It isn't like I was asking a lot from you," Flint McCall said, "or from Quincey's woman. I've been watching for several days. The passengers and the driver and shotgun guard always go inside for coffee and something to eat while you change the horses. Now, Roslyn's still a fairly pretty woman. All she has to do is hold them inside and keep them from looking at the stage. We'll tap you over the head . . . not too hard, just hard enough to make it look real. You can say that, while you were out cold, some bandits took the money box from the coach. That isn't asking too much, is it?"

I looked out at the burning hills and the heat haze writhing and shimmering. I found that my fists were clenched so tightly the nails dug into the palms of my hands.

"What if I tell you to go to hell, McCall?"

He laughed, soft and evil. "Now, you wouldn't do a thing like that, my friend. You know what would happen, don't you? I'd walk right into the house and tell old man Hardin that the son he thinks was the salt of the earth was none other than the Arapaho Kid. You wouldn't want that, would you?"

"What difference would it make?" I said. "Half the time he isn't in his right mind, anyway."

"Yes. Half the time. But what about the other half?"

"I won't do it," I said. "If you want that payroll, you'll have to stick up the stage somewhere else."

He gave that laugh again. "Quincey always said you were a strange man. Why, you think more of the old man than Quincey ever done, and you ain't even any kin. Just because he took you in and raised you . . . well, it's a good thing you feel this way, or I couldn't do business with you."

I looked him in the eye. "You say anything to Dad, and I'll kill you."

He laughed in my face. "Pshaw, now." He edged ahead on the bench so that his holstered pistol hung free, and looked pointedly at my waist where there was neither belt nor gun. I never went armed around the yard. "I rode with Quincey . . . the Arapaho Kid . . . a good many years. We rode into some tight spots, and right out of them. That mean anything to you?"

"Quincey sure rode out of the last tight spot, didn't he?" I said. "Where is he now?"

A dark look crossed his face. "He just happened to pick up a slug, that's all," he said, and shrugged. "It'll likely happen to me some day. But it won't be from you."

"I wouldn't bet on that . . . if you try anything here."

He stood up and stuck his thumbs in his belt and looked down at me with a sneer. "Full of vinegar, ain't you? Well, we'll see when the showdown comes. I've got a man keeping a watch on the stage depot in Encinal. He'll tip us off when the payroll goes out. We figure about a day or two, maybe. That gives you a little time to think. And you better think right, my friend."

I rubbed down the horses and forked some more hay into the corral. Then I saw Roslyn come out of the house and start across the yard, and I went to meet her.

"How's Dad?" I asked.

"He's napping now." She shaded her eyes with a hand and stared off across the desert in the direction Flint McCall had gone. The sun struck golden lights out of her auburn hair. "What did he want, Lew?"

I shrugged and looked away. "He just stopped to water and rest his horse."

"You know I don't believe that. He wouldn't be hanging around, if he didn't have something in mind. He brought Quincey here with the story that Quincey wanted to come home to die. Well, now Quincey's dead. What's his gang hanging around here for?"

I looked at her, and her eyes didn't waver. I thought of the box of flowers she had nurtured and placed on Quincey's grave that morning, but I knew she had done that only for Dad. What had once been in her heart had died a long time before Quincey had passed on. Sometimes I thought she loved old Dad more than I did. There was nothing else to keep her here at this lonely stage stop now that her husband was dead. There really hadn't been anything even when Quincey was alive, he had been home so seldom.

I recognized the stubborn look in her eyes, and so I told her what McCall had threatened to do. Her mouth went tight. All at once the tiny wrinkles that the burning sun and desert wind had etched into her face grew deep. She looked old now, much older than her twenty-five years.

"What are you going to do, Lew?"

"I don't know."

She couldn't resist a quick, furtive look at the house. "That's all he has left, his belief that Quincey was good and fine. If he ever learned that Quincey was the Arapaho Kid, there would be nothing left for him. We can't take everything away from him before he dies."

She was right. That was the reason we hadn't had a doctor out when Quincey had been brought home, delirious and all but dead. He'd had no other place to run to — only home, where an old man suspected nothing and only Roslyn and I knew the truth.

When Quincey had died, we'd buried him and given out the story that he'd died of a fever. Dad, with his injured, bewildered mind, had never realized that his death was caused by a gunshot wound.

I stared hard at Roslyn. "Do you want to go along with McCall, then?"

Now it was her turn to be confused and uncertain. "I don't know, Lew," she whispered.

I put a hand on her shoulder. "We've got a day or two," I said. "We'll figure out something."

"Sure," she said, but she didn't sound confident.

I looked off at the windmill, standing tall and still. The water that it pumped out of the ground was the only reason for our being here at this lonely spot between the railhead at Encinal and the mining town of Silver Hill. Nothing grew out in the barren desert sands but sage and mesquite and an occasional ocotillo.

"I think I'll grease the windmill," I said.

She turned and started for the house. Her steps were slow and thoughtful. Her head hung low.

He liked it when I put him to bed. Roslyn was always kind and gentle with him, but I suppose it was his natural sense of shame at his own helplessness that made him prefer me. I would undress him and roll him into bed and tuck the covers in. This always brought a wetness to his eyes and a tiny trembling to his mouth.

"Why, Lew?" he asked me that night.

"Why what?"

"Why do you stick around an old cripple like me?"

"Don't talk like that."

"It's true, isn't it?" He was having one of his lucid moments. Usually, he never talked like this.

I looked him in the eyes. "I was pretty helpless, too, that time you found me by the wagon train the Apaches had raided and burned."

"But that was different."

"Was it?"

"You had no one. I've got Roslyn. Anyway, she was Quincey's wife, and Quincey was my son."

"Roslyn can't go it alone. You know that."

"I wish I could do something for the two of you."

"You've already done more than enough for me," I told him gruffly, and squeezed his shoulder. "Good night, Dad."

"Good night, Lew."

Roslyn was sitting in the rocker, busy with her sewing. I paused and watched her. Feelings I couldn't express welled up in me as she threw me a long, grave look. I remembered the many nights she had sat and waited like this, her mind torn and twisted with thoughts of Quincey. And somewhere far away, Quincey was holding up a train or robbing a bank or running off cattle as the notorious Arapaho Kid. He only came home now and then, when things got too hot for him. Here in the desert country no one but Roslyn and I knew him for what he really was. At home, he could put on the dog and brag about what a success he was in the cattle-buying business, while Dad's eyes glowed with pride.

I went out into the night to see if I could find peace and forgetfulness there. As I walked toward the corrals, I heard hoof beats approaching. In the starlight I recognized the rider as the horse came to a halt in front of the house.

"Polly," I called.

She spied me, standing there by the corral, and came over to me, spurs tinkling softly in the quiet desert night.

"Hello, Lew," she said.

"What brings you out this late?"

Polly's folks ran a ranch in the foothills of the Doloritas where there was a little graze for cattle to feed on.

"You haven't been around. I've waited, but you haven't come."

All at once I felt very tired. Once I'd had a dream about her, but of late things somehow had changed, and now the dream was just another sad memory.

"I've been busy," I said, and realized on the instant that she knew I lied.

"I'm sorry for what I said to you that last time."

Hope surged in me suddenly. I was always a fool about things like that. "You've begun to see it my way, then?"

"No."

The wild, crazy hope died.

"What's there for you to be sorry about?"

She sighed. "Oh, Lew. Must you be so stubborn? It's only because I want us to have a chance. It wouldn't be fair to any of us. Don't you see?"

"You know I won't leave Dad."

She made a soft sound of exasperation. "It isn't like he'd be left with no one. He'd have Roslyn."

"But she's no kin of his. She's just Quincey's widow."

"Are you any kin?"

I didn't answer.

Polly gave that sigh again. "You don't even know who you really are. Just because he found you in that wagon train and raised you from a baby and gave you his name doesn't mean you owe him the rest of your life. You've already paid him back more than his share. What did Quincey ever do for him?"

"I don't care about Quincey."

"Oh, Lew."

"It's not like it would last forever."

"Can you name me the time? A week? A month? A year? Could you tell me just exactly how long?"

"Nobody can do that, Polly."

She caught me by the arms. Her face pressed hard against my chest, and I felt her shudder. "Oh, Lew, I just can't stand the desert. There's no future here . . . no nothing, only sun and sand and growing old and ugly before my time."

"Polly," I said. "Please try to understand."

"I understand," she said, and her voice was all bitterness. "I understand, all right, but do you? Listen to me, I'm telling you just this once. You're not the only one who's asked me to marry him. There have been many. Up to now I've said no to everyone because I love you. But do you love me?"

"You know I do."

"Enough to take me away from here?"

I was silent.

"Bob Nesbitt will," she said quietly.

"Nesbitt?" I echoed. He owned a livery and feed business in Encinal. "Do you mean it?"

"All I have to do is say yes, and he'll sell his business and take me away, anywhere I want to go. I promised to give him my answer tomorrow night."

"Polly," I said desperately, all at once wanting her very much and seeing only loneliness and remorse, if I ever lost her, "just give me a little more time. There's something come up. A week. Give me that, won't you?"

"Tomorrow night," she said in a voice that told me there was no arguing.

Roslyn glanced up at me, sharp and hard, when I went back to the house.

"It was only Polly," I said.

She didn't say anything. She just went on rocking. All at once all the wretchedness in the world swept over me.

I whispered with anguish: "I don't know what I'd do if I lost her."

"Go to her, then."

I couldn't help a quick glance at the room where Dad slept. Roslyn noticed, and her eyes softened.

"I'll manage," she said gently. "It won't be too hard. After all, you've got your life to live."

"What about you?"

"My life has already been lived. The best part of it has been lived." Her eyes came back to me and pleaded with me. "Go to her, Lew."

I shook my head. "I'll never leave him."

Two tears gathered on her lashes. "You owe it to yourself, Lew."

"I owe him more."

"What about McCall?"

That snapped me out of it. All at once I was through being sorry for myself. McCall. I felt the hate rise and storm in me. Then it died in the face of my helplessness.

"I don't know," I said.

"How much time do we have?"

"A day. Two, at the most."

"Are you going along with McCall?"

"Do you want me not to?"

Her glance wavered and fell. "I don't know."

A sudden pity for her filled me. She had had more than her share of grief, and it was not yet over. It would never be over for her. Memory of that grave outside and of the man in it would dog her to her dying day. I went over and put a hand on her shoulder and squeezed. She glanced up at me with a quick, warm look.

"There's coffee on the stove, Lew," she said. "I kept it warm for you."

Somewhere out in the desert night a coyote wailed, and another answered. Lonely, haunting sounds.

The instant the sun rose next morning, it began to singe the sage and greasewood. A small, hot wind began to blow, stirring up tiny dust devils that swirled and skipped across the yard.

I stood, watching the road from Encinal, looking for a dust cloud that would tell the approach of riders, but only the desert was there, burnt and barren under the yellow sky. Roslyn came and stood beside me. I glanced at her and saw that she was watching the road, too, with one hand shading her eyes.

"Maybe it won't be today," I told her. "Maybe it won't be until tomorrow."

"What's the difference?" she said wearily. "I'd just as soon have it happen today and get it over with." Her eyes probed at me. "Did you decide anything yet?"

"What could I decide?"

"Then you're going along with McCall?"

I didn't answer.

She gave my arm a squeeze. "Whatever you do is all right with me," she said. And then she was gone, her footsteps whispering like lost secrets across the yard.

I heard a far-off drum of racing hoofs. My first glad thought was that the stage was coming at last, but then it dawned on me that the sounds were just the running hoof beats of horses and riders.

I crossed the yard and stood there, watching them ride up. There were three of them. Flint McCall rode in the lead, and behind him were the two others that I had seen the time they had brought Quincey home. I remembered their names — Wind River and Jesse Brackins.

They pulled up in a swirl of dust, and I heard the door open behind me and knew Roslyn was standing there. Then came the soft *tap-tapping* of Dad's cane.

"Quincey?" his trembling query came. "Is that Quincey, come home at last, Roslyn?"

"Hush, Dad," she said in a tight voice.

"Quincey?" he asked again. "I don't see so good. Is that Quincey there?"

"No, Dad. It isn't Quincey."

He made a small, choking sound of apology. "That's right. Quincey's dead. I keep forgetting."

McCall was grinning as he listened.

"I'd chew the fat with you, Hardin," he growled, "but there isn't time. The stage will be here soon. You make up your mind yet what you're going to do?"

"Go inside, Roslyn," I said. "Take Dad and go inside . . . and stay there."

"Lew?" Dad said. "Is something wrong?" I could tell from his voice that he was going to have one of his lucid moments.

"Get him inside." I snapped the words at Roslyn.

The cane tapped, shoes whispered, and the door closed. McCall began to grin.

"I'm glad to see you so sensible, my friend," he said, smiling. "Now we ain't got much time. We've got to hide." His eyes scanned the barn by the corrals. He nodded. "That should do the trick."

We waited inside, the four of us. While we waited, McCall told me what to do.

"You go out first like you always do," he said, "and change teams. As soon as everyone is in the house, me and Brackins will take care of the money box. You make sure you come back here where Wind River will give you a little tap on the head to make things look right. Wind River will have a gun on you all the while. You make one wrong move, and he'll let you have it. He don't miss. He's our best shot, even better than me, even better than the Arapaho Kid. You got it clear now?"

"I got it clear," I growled.

We were in the dimness of the haymow, watching the yard outside through the open door. McCall leaned lazily on the handle of a pitchfork stuck in the hay. Brackins stood beside him. Wind River stood behind me. He was the only one holding a gun. The others didn't have to.

Brackins was the first to see the dust cloud in the distance. He announced it in a sharp, low voice to McCall. McCall grinned and hitched up his shell belt. Wind River edged ahead to take a look, then dropped back quickly behind me again. The hand that held his pistol was like a rock.

The sounds the stage made pulling in were like the rumble of the world, tumbling down about my ears.

McCall gave me a vicious dig in the ribs with his elbow and whispered harshly: "Get the hell out there . . . and quick!"

There were no passengers, just the driver and the shotgun guard. I seemed to be walking in a dream. I answered their greetings in words I can't recall. They didn't suspect anything. Roslyn called to them from the gallery, and they went there, laughing and joshing her.

I got the tired, sweating horses unhitched and the fresh team in their place. The driver and the guard were inside by now, and McCall and Brackins came trotting out of the barn. I led the tired team into the barn.

All at once I had had enough. *You're no better than Quincey,* something said to me. *You're doing what Quincey always did. What if Dad ever finds out the truth about this? If nothing else, he's always had you and Roslyn, but she's in this along with you. If he ever learns the truth, then he'll have nothing for the little time left.*

I stopped and leaned back and threw a quick look outside. "Who's that out there?" I cried.

Wind River caught the sharpness in my voice and stepped ahead and threw a look around the edge of the doorway. In that instant I grabbed the pitchfork that was stuck into the hay and plunged the tines of the fork into his chest.

He screamed, and his gun blasted, but the barrel was tilted high, and the recoil bounced it out of his grasp. As he went crashing down on his side, I scooped up the pistol and jumped to the door.

I shot Brackins as he was climbing down from the coach. He went sprawling in the dust and never moved. McCall fiddled an instant with the money box, but it was too heavy for him, and by then the horses were plunging and shying in fright. The dust they raised half hid McCall from sight. I threw two shots at him as he broke for the shelter of a corner of the house, just as the driver and the guard came bursting out the door.

I thought I saw McCall stagger as he rounded the corner out of sight. Then he began to shout.

"Old man!" McCall cried at the top of his lungs. "Do you hear me? I've got something to tell you. About your son, your Quincey. Listen good, old man. Your Quincey. . . ."

I was almost at the corner of the house. I didn't care any

more, if he shot me down. I wanted only to stop him before the harm was done. Then one shot rang out, and his words died in his throat.

He was down, with his face pushed against the earth. Roslyn gave one little cry and dropped her rifle, with the smoke still trickling out of the barrel. She covered her face with her hands and started to weep.

She told me about it that evening after sunset, after we had put Dad to bed. She told me how, at the first shot, she had grabbed the rifle, and, when she had seen McCall going around the corner of the house, she had circled it in the opposite direction. As he crouched below a window, she had shot him.

She shuddered and put her face in her hands. "It was murder," she said.

I patted the auburn head gently. "Someone else will judge that," I said. "It's out of our hands."

She looked up at me now with a keen, searching stare. "Go to Polly, Lew, while you still have time."

I shook my head.

"McCall is dead," she went on. "They're all dead who knew about Quincey. I can handle things now. Go to her."

"I'm staying with you," I said. "Even after Dad goes, I'm staying with you. If you'll have me, Roslyn."

The smile she showed me then was dazzling. "What a silly thing to ask," she said.

Dad called to us then, and with our arms around each other we went to him.

Witch

He had never shot a man in cold blood before, and, even though it was over, the sick feeling that had formed in his stomach the instant before he'd pressed the trigger still persisted. He tried comforting himself by thinking that it was only an Indian, an Apache at that, and, if he hadn't killed the man, the girl would be dead instead, but the thought gave him little solace.

She knelt on the ground, making small, lamenting sounds over the owl that the Apache had killed with his first shot. That would have been all right, he told himself, and he'd have ridden away from what he'd stumbled upon, but, when the Apache had drawn a bead on the girl, he'd jerked his pistol and shot the Indian dead.

He rode the coyote dun up to the girl. The yellow horse made hardly any sound as though respecting the death and grief that existed here. The girl was Apache, too, and the long hair glistened blue-black in the sun. Her clothing was of antelope skin, and there was a beaded band about her forehead.

She did not look up, although she must be aware of him and the horse. She went on mourning over the owl that lay bloody with feathers awry.

His stomach seemed a little better now; his heart was back to its normal beat. He even found a moment to remember the hunters on his trail and to wonder if they had heard the shots. But he was sure they were too far behind for that. He reckoned he had a good day's lead on them, perhaps two, unless they'd guessed his destination and had cut across country to intercept him. A little angrily he put these thoughts from his mind. It was something he would have to grow accustomed to — this being hunted. He was well aware of the relentless nature of the men who were after him.

"It's all right," he said to the girl. "He can't hurt you any more."

Her soft lamentations stopped. She looked up at him, and he could tell she had not understood him. So he tried Spanish which some of the Apache tribes knew.

"He is dead," he said. "You have nothing to fear from him any more."

She rose to her feet. She was young, he thought, about his own age which was twenty, and quite pretty. There was a lithe grace in each movement, a touch of the primitive and untamed.

"I have no fear," she said with a pride that was almost scorn. "Apaches do not know fear."

It made him smile to hear this from a young and pretty girl, and then he remembered the stories he'd heard of the Apache torture stakes. It was said that the women and girls were even more skilled than the warriors at inflicting agony. The whole Southwest breathed easier now that Geronimo and his braves had been deported to Florida and the rest of the Apaches were confined to reservations. This made him think of something.

"Which reservation are you from?"

"Mimbreño."

"Why are you not there?"

"They would have killed me."

"Who?"

"My people."

"Why?"

"Because I am a witch. . . ."

* * * * *

Thinking back on her words about being a witch, he found them quite funny. It was a good thing for him, he told himself, this finding of something to divert his mind from his own troubles. He had become almost obsessed with memories of the San Martín Cattle War, and the day he'd been forced to shoot young Grover Greene, and the need to run and keep on running, because old Abijah Greene and a couple of his hired guns were on his trail.

She sensed his mirth even though he did not show it, and he could tell that she resented it. A dark look entered her eyes, and for a moment he was uneasy, for she wore a knife in a beaded sheath at her waist. Then he told himself she was only a girl. He could handle her.

They had camped for the night. The fire crackled, and for a few instants he allowed himself to dream of the morrow. *Allison,* he thought with a great and hungry yearning. *Allison.* Then he put her image from him and looked at the Apache girl. He had told her she could accompany him as far as Dos Santos which they would reach tomorrow. Somehow he felt a certain responsibility toward her, and he could not understand this. Was it perhaps because he had saved her life?

"How are you called?" he asked.

"Lahneen."

"I am Les Nathan."

"Na-than." She made two words out of the name.

He stared across the fire at her, and an urge to tease came over him. "You are quite young and pretty to be a witch, are you not?"

The dark eyes grew darker. "You are making fun of me. You are mocking me."

"I am only saying what you told me."

"You do not believe I am a witch? Why would my people want to kill me, if I was not one?"

"How does one know that a person is a witch?"

"Did you not see the owl?"

He remembered the bird, lying dead, and the sad sounds she had made over it.

"Among my people an owl is a sign of misfortune. It is an omen that is much feared. I have always liked to make pets of animals. When I found the owl with an injured wing, I cared for it in secret until it was well. But then one day outside my *jacal* it flew from nowhere and lit on my shoulder. This was seen, and that was the sign to my people that I was a witch."

"Even if your people think you a witch, that is not reason enough for them to kill you."

"The man you shot, Kanseah, he said I was the cause of the death of his son."

"Were you?" he asked.

She was watching the play of the flames. "I do not know. Soon after the day the owl flew on my shoulder and I was told to leave the village, the son of Kanseah came down with a great pain in his belly and then died. I was warned by a friend that Kanseah had sworn he would kill the owl and then me. So I fled the reservation, but Kanseah followed."

He was silent, thinking. She sounded sincere. He had a searing recollection of the bullet hitting the owl, sending feathers flying, and of the Indian then drawing a bead on the girl. It was only superstition, this matter of the owl being bad luck, but he knew that Indians took such things seriously.

He became aware that she was watching him. "You do not believe me," she said.

"I believe you. It is only that I do not believe in witches."

"Are there no witches among the White Eyes?"

"There are women who wear long, black dresses and rings in their ears and who say they can foretell the future in the lines in the palm of one's hand. Only we do not call them witches. We call them Gypsies."

"You are laughing at me." There was angry accusation in her tone, although the round face remained inscrutable. "I do not need to look at your hands to foretell your future."

"No? What, then, is my future?"

"You are to die. Soon."

The laughter was already bubbling in his throat, when he remembered old Abijah Greene and Laredo and Chip Hart. Merriment fled. A chill embraced his shoulders.

Her eyes were upon him like the stare of death. "You will die," she said again. "Before too many sleeps."

They rode out of the Pinnacles early in the afternoon, and there ahead of them lay the buildings of Calvin Tyler's ranch. He could feel the quickened beating of his heart, the cloying rush of anticipation. It irritated him to have the Indian girl riding behind him in the fashion of a squaw following her brave.

He waved an arm toward the south. "Dos Santos is there. You'll come across a creek and that will take you to the town. I am not going to Dos Santos. I have . . . ah . . . business here."

She said nothing. She watched him with dark, inscrutable eyes. She made no move to start her pony.

"Well, good bye, Lahneen," he said, and touched spurs to the coyote dun.

Tyler's dog set up a racket, but he called the animal's name. Then, all at once, the dog remembered and came to greet him with great bounds and a furious wagging of its tail. He dismounted and fondled the dog's ears, and, when he looked up, he saw her running to meet him, blonde hair aglow in the sun.

"Allison," he said, folding the sweetness of her in his embrace. Then his throat was all choked up, and the rush of words that had built up in him had to remain unspoken.

Her lips trembled on his, and he drew back to study her face. "Tears?" he said gently. "Why?"

"I worried so much for you, Les."

"I told you I'd be careful. I told you I'd look out for myself."

"But it was such a vicious war. We heard all the stories that came out of San Martín County. I feared for you so."

All at once he was aware of the weight of the pistol in the holster at his hip. Remembrance came of the distaste and remorse after he had shot young Grover Greene and of the sick sensation in his stomach when he'd killed the Apache, Kanseah. He wished he could lay that gun aside, but he dared not do that as long as those three hunted him, and they were relentless enough to hound him the rest of his life.

He stroked the blonde head and smiled down at the tear-stained face. "It's going to be different from now on," he said, hoping she wouldn't read the lie in his words. "I've had my fill of gunfighting. All I want to do is settle down."

"Oh, Les. Do you mean that?" Her face lit up with a happiness he'd never seen there before. Then her glance went past him, and he saw the frown and look of disapproval. "Who's that?"

He turned. The Indian girl was there on her pony, face expressionless, wind swirling her long black hair. He knew a burst of irritation and anger.

"I thought you were going on to Dos Santos. What are you doing here?"

"I have no wish to go to Dos Santos."

"Go somewhere else, then."

"My horse is thirsty. I wish to give him a drink."

"There is water in that creek I told you about."

"I may not wish to ride in that direction."

"Who is she?" Allison Tyler asked.

"Just someone I. . . ." Then he grinned. "A witch."

"Les Nathan. You are not one bit funny."

"It's true, Allison. Why, she even foretold my. . . ." He caught himself, and the laughter died coldly in him. He watched the Indian girl ride past and on to the tank by the clanking windmill.

Allison Tyler was peering up at his face. "Foretold what?"

"Nothing. Just Indian superstition. She had to leave her reservation because her people believed she had put a curse on them. They were ready to kill her. I came upon her, and, since we were going in the same direction, she rode with me." He did not mention the Apache he had killed. It was bad enough that Allison knew about Grover Greene.

Allison drew back from him and watched the Indian girl watering her pony. It came to Les Nathan that all the joy had gone from him. In its place was a dismal chill like a musty breath from a tomb.

Calvin Tyler's thick-lensed spectacles gave his eyes an owlish look. Owlish, Les Nathan thought, and remembered the dead owl and Lahneen and her prophecy for him. Something akin to panic chattered in him, and he dismissed it angrily. A lot of superstitious foolishness. He was not going to let it get him.

Calvin Tyler's voice was soft but firm. They were alone

in the parlor of Tyler's home. Allison was somewhere outside. Tyler spoke with a frequent clearing of his throat, as though something bothersome kept lodging there.

"I tried to warn you, Les. I tried to reason with you, but you wouldn't listen. I told you to stay out of that business in San Martín County."

"I only did it for Allison, Mister Tyler. You know I've always been fixing to marry her. They were paying good wages in San Martín."

"Gun wages," Tyler said, and cleared his throat.

"Where else could I have drawn wages like that?"

"Blood money," Tyler said.

Nathan felt his face get warm. "If you mean Grover Greene, Mister Tyler, I was forced into it. When he braced me, I had no choice. It was either draw against him or run, and I ain't the running kind."

"What're you doing right now?" Tyler asked softly.

Nathan had a vision of old Abijah Greene and Laredo and Chip Hart. He knew what Calvin Tyler meant, and it started a resentment building in him.

"I'm sick of killing," he said. "I'm running not because I'm scared of them, but because, if they corner me, I'll fight back and try to get as many of them as I can before they get me, even though I don't want to kill any more. I ain't yellow, Mister Tyler. I just don't want no more trouble."

"I'm sorry, Les. I didn't mean it that way." The owl eyes peered at Nathan, and he felt that chill travel across his shoulders again. "You still aiming to marry my Allison?"

"I am."

"Even though you're a hunted man?"

"It isn't like I was an outlaw. The only reason old Abijah Greene is after me is because I was on the losing side. If we had won, nothing would be done about me shooting down his son, because it was just plain self-defense."

Tyler cleared his throat. "I believe you, son, but that don't mean Abijah Greene is going to stop tracking you."

"I know. That's why I want to marry Allison and then travel on."

"How far?"

"I don't know. Pretty far. California, maybe. Or clear up to Montana. Or maybe even Canada."

"You think you can ever get far enough away from Abijah Greene?"

He could feel the pulse pounding in his throat. He realized full well the enormity of what lay ahead, and this insistent questioning was beginning to anger him.

"I can try," he said sullenly.

"Meanwhile, what about my Allison? I suppose you'll be taking her with you, since she'll be your wife?"

He sensed defeat then, and the knowledge left him empty of words. He could only sit and stare at the floor.

Tyler went on. "I love my Allison, Les. I want her to be happy with the man she marries. I want her to have a good life. What would it be like for her, running every time you run, looking over her shoulder every time you look over yours, coming awake full of fear at night, always listening for the sound of hoof beats behind, watching the horizon for sight of Abijah Greene or his men. Have you ever thought of that, Les?"

He knew now how it was going to be, and for an instant he wished that Abijah and Laredo and Chip Hart would be there in the yard, waiting, when he stepped out of the house, just to get it over with, just to die, since there was not much to living without Allison. A sorrow such as he had never known came over him.

"Let her be, Les," Tyler was saying. "If you really love

her, if you really want to do right by her, you'll leave without even saying good bye."

"Not even good bye?" he cried. "Why, she'd hate me the rest of her life, if I did that."

"In the long run it would be easier for her, son, hating you. Loving you, she would just pine away. You wouldn't want that, would you?"

"But I love her, Mister Tyler. I love Allison."

"I know. But how much? This is your chance to show how much."

He stood, tense and apprehensive, behind the outcropping of rock, with a hand clamped over the coyote dun's nostrils so that the horse could not whinny as the three riders passed on the trail below. His heart was going with such hard hammer strokes that he was sure they would hear it. But they rode on without a glance above and headed down the western flank of the Pinnacles toward the Tyler Ranch in the distance.

For a moment he felt like ripping the rifle out of its saddle scabbard and shooting them down with as little pity as they would show him, when they finally caught him. But then he remembered the Apache he had shot without warning, and the way his stomach had turned, and how he felt sick again just thinking about it. So he let them ride on without a hint that he was there, and then he got on the dun and loped off in the opposite direction.

When he first heard the horse behind him, he was sure it was they, and he reined the dun around sharply, the pistol whipping up in his hand. With his finger already starting to press the trigger, he saw who it was, and he clamped his thumb down on the hammer just in time to keep the gun from going off.

"Lahneen," he said, "what are you doing here?"

She stared at him with no emotion on her features. "I have no wish to go to Dos Santos or beyond. So I am returning."

"To the reservation?"

"Perhaps."

"But they will kill you, if you return there. You said. . . ." He broke off in anger. It was all silly superstition and foolishness, and here he was accepting it as though it were immutable fact. He slid the pistol back in its holster and regarded her with a baleful stare. "Why are you following me?"

"I follow no one. I happen to be riding in the same direction as you, that is all."

"I do not want you with me. Go."

He thought he saw a glint of interest, of searching in the dark eyes, but it could have been a trick of the waning light after sunset.

"Why are you here, Na-than?" she asked. "I had thought you would stay with her of the yellow hair."

"I am not wanted," he said bitterly. "I am not wanted anywhere."

"I saw the three White Eyes," she said. "I saw how you hid from them. Are they your enemies, Na-than?"

"None of your damned business!" he said, and was instantly glad he had spoken in English. He felt irritable, miserable. He wanted to be alone, to die alone, without tears, without mourning. The thought of dying made him wonder. Was she following him to see the fulfillment of her prophecy?

Wrath swirled anew in him. "Go," he said in Spanish. "*Andale.*"

She did not stir. Her face betrayed no emotion.

He was in no mood for further talking, further argument. It would only be a matter of time before Abijah Greene and Laredo and Chip Hart reached Tyler's ranch and, not finding him there, doubled back. He had to concern himself with survival, not a silly, superstitious savage. He whirled the dun and, without another word, rode off.

He dared not risk a fire and made a cold camp. The mountain air was chill, but it was not this that kept him awake most of the night. It was the memories, the regret and reproach. *Allison, Allison.* He had thought that she would follow. Now he had to face the bitter truth. She did not love him, else she would be here with him. Apparently she preferred the security of her father's home to the uncertainty and ordeal of a fugitive's life. He should have seen that selfishness in her from the start. Then the truth wouldn't be so hard and aching to accept.

When he awoke in the morning, he felt more tired than the night before and knew this was the result of his restless, dream-tossed sleep. He saddled the coyote dun, then found he was reluctant to mount and ride on. A faint, dismal hope held him here. Perhaps the night had changed her mind. Perhaps she had needed the cover of darkness to steal away from her father. If this were so, and he rode on and did not wait for her, he would be at fault.

Indecision angered him. Recollection of the three men he had seen the day before came, and he knew that, if he valued his life, he should be moving on. But he could not bring himself to abandon the last, sweet memory he had left.

The sound of an approaching horse startled him, brought him around on a heel, hand on his pistol. Then he remembered that they were three and this was but a single horse. Still, his hand stayed on the gun.

Allison? His heart began to race at the thought.

It was the Indian girl.

He hoped the disgust and anger he was sure were evident on his face would drive her away, but she simply sat on the pony and stared at him with the calm that irritated him so.

"Are you still around?" he growled. "Did I not tell you I did not want you with me any more?"

"You did not sleep last night, did you, Na-than?" There was a strange gentleness in her voice, an odd softness in the obsidian eyes. "Are you not well?"

He swung angrily up in the saddle. "There is nothing wrong with me." His baleful glance rested on her. "Why do you keep following me?"

"I have no other place to go."

"Is it to see if your prophecy will come true?"

"Poor Na-than. I said those words in anger. I did not mean to frighten you."

"I am not frightened. I am not afraid of death. I do not want you around, that is all."

"I would like to help you, Na-than."

"Then ride on. Go. *Andale*. I want no more to lay eyes on you."

She stared at him a while without emotion. Then she turned the pony and rode away. He watched her go, happy and pleased at first, but, some time after she was gone, a dim feeling of melancholy and aloneness came over him. He told himself this was because the Pinnacles were such a lonely, isolated mountain range.

He saw first the dust, a thin spiral of it rising like a beacon or a warning of doom. They had picked up his tracks; they were onto him at last. He urged the coyote dun to a faster pace, thinking to outdistance them, since the dun was still fresh and their mounts would be weary. Then he remembered the prophecy.

Can a man outrun his fate? The futility of it hit him like a blow. By fleeing he would only prolong the torment. He might as well stand and face the inevitable.

He came across a cluster of rocks and decided this was as good a chance as any. Dismounting, he stood and looked around a while, thinking wryly that this was to be his tomb. It really did not matter where a man died, he told himself, but how well. He would give as good an account of himself as he could. No one could ask more than that.

He got his rifle, and then lay down on his belly to wait for them. Now that the time for killing was again at hand, he felt that cold knot forming in his stomach anew. The enormity of his mistakes descended on him, and he felt that his impending death was just retribution for the deaths he had dealt. It had been wrong to hire out his gun. He should have realized that before he had killed young Grover Greene, not after. He was reaping what he had sown. Had the Indian girl known that?

Now that he thought about it, he found that the prophecy was not so remarkable, after all. It was most apparent that he was marked for violent death, and soon. He was only one; they were three. He was still a novice in the ways of violence, even though he had tasted blood, while they were old and cunning in the ways of dealing death. So it was quite obvious that he would soon die. Calvin Tyler had foreseen that and sent him packing before he brought tragedy to Allison. But how could the Indian girl have known? Had she seen something in his eyes and face? Or was she truly a witch with supernatural power?

A sharp whinny from the dun brought him out of his

thinking, all at once alert, eyes searching the land ahead, and he saw a horseman emerge from a stand of jumpers and ride directly for him. Only one rider, old, shriveled, white mustache and goatee standing out like new snow on a mountain peak.

He looked all about, swiftly, suspiciously, but there was just the one horseman. He aimed the rifle. "That's far enough, Abijah," he called out.

It was as though the old man had not heard. He came on.

"I said that's far enough," Nathan cried, and sent a warning shot over the old man's head.

"Save your cartridges, boy," Abijah Greene said, but he reined in and dismounted. He started in on foot, walking with calm deliberation for the rock cluster.

"I mean it, Abijah." Sweat stood out above Nathan's lip. "I'll drop you, if you keep coming."

"You know I'm not armed, boy," the old man said. He spread his coat wide to show he spoke the truth. "I never carried a weapon in all my life. Guns only get a body in trouble, as you well know, boy."

"Not one more step, Abijah."

Something in Nathan's tone halted the old man. He rose on tiptoes to peer over the rock behind which Nathan lay.

"Put that gun away, boy. You make me nervous."

"That's all right with me."

"I just want to talk with you."

"What about?"

This encouraged the old man. He took a step ahead, then halted anew as Nathan moved the rifle menacingly.

"I want you to come home with me, son."

Nathan laughed.

The old man edged another half step ahead, then

stopped. "I mean it, boy," he said. "I'm lonely with my Grover gone . . . lonely. I had great plans for my boy, but he's gone." He raised a hand and passed it over his eyes. "You're about my Grover's age. I want you to take his place, son."

"How stupid do you think I am, Abijah?"

"I mean it, boy. I . . . there's nothing for me to live for any more, no one to leave my land to, my herds. I'm a forgiving man, son. You'll see, if only you'll give me the chance. I warned Grover. He who lives by the gun dies by the gun. That's what I told my Grover, but he was headstrong. He wouldn't listen. Now he's dead. You know I don't hold with guns. That's why I'm always unarmed."

"You don't need to wear a gun because you've always had others do your killing for you," Nathan said. "Where's Laredo and Chip Hart, Abijah?"

The old man waved a hand vaguely. "I sent them away."

"You expect me to believe that?"

"It's the Gospel truth, son. I figured you'd be jumpy . . . would have the wrong idea about me. So to make sure there'd be no trouble, I sent them on their way."

Nathan got up on an elbow for a swift scanning of the land all around, and Greene moved in another step. Nathan put the sights of the rifle back on the old man's breast.

"If this is a trick, Abijah," Nathan said, "you're as good as dead."

"No trick, son. Please come home with me. Don't let me spend my last days all alone."

From somewhere behind Nathan came a sound, the low, mourning call of an owl. Greene heard it, too, and his head flung up in sudden alarm. Then a gun blasted, just as Nathan was coming around. The slug ricocheted off a rock, chipping tiny shards that stung Nathan's cheek and made him blink with pain. And then he saw them, charging him from the rear, where they had deployed while the old man kept him occupied with beguiling talk.

He sent burly Laredo tumbling with his first shot, missed waspy Chip Hart with the second, but dropped him with the third. Then something exploded with a barb of pain on the back of his neck, and his rifle fell. He started to pitch forward, trying to roll at the same time to get a view of Abijah Greene, and he landed on the stone with which Greene had struck him. Fumbling fingers found the grip of his pistol, as the old one leaped ahead to snatch up the rifle, and, even as he raised the pistol, Nathan knew he was too late.

The rifle blasted, and the world was a mass of agony. As the red abyss yawned, he thought he heard a screech of anguish from the old man, but that couldn't be — the screech must be his own as he plunged downward.

It had been like a journey to the grave and back. He could not believe he was still alive. He must have died and then been born again. The aching in his head was the pain of rebirth.

Her fingers were gentle, as they touched the bullet crease on the side of his skull in bandaging it. "Poor Na-than," she said once, and he looked at her and saw solicitude on what had once been an aloof, expressionless face.

He glanced about and saw all three of them dead — Laredo and Chip Hart by his bullets, the old man by the knife of the girl. It came to Nathan then that the need to run, the need to kill was gone. He knew he would never again use a gun on a fellow man. That part of his life was dead, that part of him was dead. The man who remained was distinctly different and alien to the man of the old, violence-ridden days. So she had been right about his death, after all — the death of Les Nathan, gunfighter.

She was done now and rose to her feet.

"Where are you going?" he asked.

She would not face him. "You told me you did not want me around you any more. I would not have returned, except that I saw the White Eyes and knew they meant to kill you. I warned you with the call of the owl and helped you because you saved my life. Now there is no more need for me."

"There is much need," he said.

He saw the slim shoulders straighten, the dark head lift. But she did not turn around.

"There will be need for you the rest of my life, Lahneen."

She turned then and came and sat down in front of him, and, when she showed him her first smile, it was the whitest, brightest thing Les Nathan had ever seen.

Dark Purpose

Joe Garth had convinced himself over the past two years that tears would no longer move him, but he knew now that firmly held belief had been an illusion. He knew it from the way his heart pained and from the way a faint melancholy had started in him. He stood and listened, while the world and the pattern of his days ended and a new world and a new pattern took ominous shape.

"I don't know who else to ask," Jill was saying, while the tears glistened and trembled on her lashes in bright sunlight. "I don't know where to turn. All I could think of was you, Joe."

She had been very pretty once, a scant two years before. She was still attractive, but the sorrow of existence was having its way with her. Its cruel mark lay in the fine lines at the edges of her eyes and in the even sharper lines at the corners of her mouth. Shadows haunted the depths of her eyes. The skin was drawn tightly over her cheekbones.

"I don't know what I can do," he said as gently as he could. "I don't know what anybody could do."

"They mean to kill him. They don't mean to take him alive. But if someone got to him and talked to him?"

To avoid the anguished pleading in her eyes, he turned his stare on the far distances. "This is big country, Jill," he said quietly. "There are more than two hundred men hunting him. He knows the woods . . . he knows them as well as any man. They may never find him."

"But he can't hold out forever. Not with the heat, the

mosquitoes, and hardly any food. Len Uhle will find him. You're just lying to spare me."

"I know," Garth said.

"Won't you do something, then? Won't you at least try to do something?"

"There just simply isn't anything I can do, Jill."

She put her face in her hands, and the tears became audible now. Her shoulders shook, her whole body contorted with anguish.

"Jill," he said pleadingly. It took an effort to keep from touching her. He wanted so much to put an arm around her, to comfort her, to ease her tears. But he knew he would be sorry, that it could lead only to aching memories and regret.

"Two men have already died because of me," she said. "If he's killed, his death will be my fault, too. It would live and walk with me as long as I live."

"You?" he asked softly. He felt something move darkly in him, a portent of dread and evil.

Her sobs stilled, and she looked up at him. Tears still trembled on her lashes, but her eyes were bright with defiance. Color touched the high points of her cheeks. "Don't you know why Roy killed Crawford and Erdman?"

He frowned. "Uhle deputized them to arrest Roy on some game charges. He shot Erdman first, then Crawford while Crawford was trying to run away."

"Does that make sense?" she asked. "Killing two men because they wanted to arrest him for something as trivial as that? No, Joe. He waited for them and then killed them deliberately. He knew exactly what he was doing."

He stared at her without speaking. He was thinking, remembering.

"You know what Crawford was," she said. "You know

how he talked about me, about all women."

"I think Roy knew him as well as any of us. I would say he'd take that into consideration."

"Still he hated Crawford. Deliberately."

A chill moved clammily along Garth's shoulder blades. "Did he have just cause?"

Her defiance fled. Shame bowed her head and made her look small and helpless, and alone. She nodded.

"I never thought of you in that way," he said quietly, sadly. "All the while I've known you, I never thought of you as the kind of woman who would. . . ." He let the words trail off.

"Let's say I've changed," she said without looking up. "Oh, Joe, I can't talk about it. Please don't make me talk about it." She began to cry again.

"All right," he said, "I won't. Don't cry any more."

She lifted haunted eyes to him. Her sobs had ceased, but the tears still trickled crookedly down her cheeks. "Will you help me, Joe?"

He stared at her without speaking, gripped by helplessness, feeling empty and hollow again.

"For me? For the old days? We had some good times in the old days. Can you forgive me enough to help me?"

He knew it was wrong — all the way. There was nothing he could gain from it but anguish and sorrow and possibly even death. Still he said: "All right, Jill. I'll do what I can."

The two men had rifles, and they stepped out into the middle of the gravel road and waved Garth's car to a stop. Somewhere in the forest nearby a yellowhammer called, loud and ringing, as Joe Garth poked his head out the window.

One of the men was quite young, hardly more than a boy.

The rifle and his temporary importance made him swagger a bit. "You've got to turn back, buddy," he said. "This is a roadblock."

"Is that right?" Garth said.

"We figure Roy Anderson's somewhere around here. No one's using this road past this spot."

Garth stared at the green, impenetrable face of the forest, his lips tightening. "I suppose Anderson will use the road if he comes by," he said, his voice brittle with irony. "*If* he comes by. . . ."

"I got my orders," the boy said. "Anderson could fit in my trunk. You got to be real careful, bub."

The other man came up. He was tall and stringy with a sour, whisker-studded face. "All right, all right," he said to Garth. "He's just a kid. Stop riding him. And turn around and go back."

"Is Uhle up ahead?"

Gray eyes squinted hard at Garth. "You a deputy?"

"Something like that."

"Where's your badge?"

"Where's yours?" Garth asked.

"I've had just about enough of your lip."

"Look," Garth said with impatience and weariness, "there just aren't enough badges to go around. You'd need over two hundred. That's why you and the kid don't have any . . . and I don't. I've got to see Sheriff Uhle. Is he up ahead?"

The posseman chewed his lip while he thought, his eyes screwed almost shut in concentration. Finally he said: "O K. Go on."

The road skirted a small lake glistening like a deep-blue sapphire in the hot sunlight and plunged into a stand of white birch. It climbed a rather steep hill and dipped sharply down the other side and curved to cross a ravine on a wooden bridge. The river beneath was very calm.

This was resort country. Cabins and lodges nestled on the shores of the many lakes, some of them open to view, others hidden in clandestine remoteness. The forest passing by held out a false invitation of coolness and comfort, revealing nothing of the mosquitoes that swarmed in the swampy lowlands and infested the shores of the lakes at night.

Garth saw the cars parked near the abandoned lodge and the men standing about. He pulled off the road and got out. Eyes picked him up and examined him, one pair sharper and more hostile than all the rest.

Garth felt a surge of animosity, of mutual dislike. But he kept his face calm and blank. His stride was unhurried, casual. He nodded to several men he knew and received nods in return.

"How'd you get here?" Sheriff Len Uhle asked. He was a florid, handsome man with dark, brooding eyes. He was starting to thicken about the waist.

"There's my car," Garth said, nodding toward the lodge.

"How'd you get past the roadblock?"

"I told them I wanted to see you."

"About what?"

"Nothing. That was just an excuse."

Uhle's big hands flexed, the long, thick fingers curling into fists and clenching tightly as though crushing an invisible something to nothingness. His eyes burned with the rage and turmoil seething within him. But his voice remained coldly matter-of-fact.

"Why have you come?" he demanded.

"To help Anderson."

"Someday, Garth, you're going to get a little too smart for your own good." He beckoned sharply. "Come on. You and me are going to have a little talk."

Uhle led the way to Garth's car. Uhle glanced inside, noting the .30-30 on the back seat. Something glimmered in his eyes as he returned Garth's impassive stare.

"I could make trouble for you, Garth," he said, "for carrying a loaded gun in your car."

"I'm not the only one these days," Garth said.

"The others have been deputized. You haven't."

"How about deputizing me, then?"

Uhle showed a grin, toothy, contemptuous. "Go to hell," he said.

"You need all the men you can get, don't you?"

"I don't need you, Garth."

"What have you got against me?"

"Plenty," Uhle snarled. "I've never liked you, and you've never liked me. You sounded off plenty during election time against me, and you've sounded off plenty since. I've no use for you. So get in your car and get the hell away from here."

"This is a free country."

"How come your sudden interest in catching Anderson, Garth? Tell me that."

"I'm a law-abiding citizen," Garth said dryly. "It's my duty."

A sly, ugly look came into Uhle's eyes. "I remember now. You were sweet on Anderson's wife once, weren't you? But she married him, instead. You haven't looked at another woman since. Yes. I can see why you'd like Anderson taken care of."

"Like you took care of Crawford and Erdman?" Garth said.

"Just exactly what do you mean by that?"

"How come you sent Crawford and Erdman to arrest Roy? They weren't even regular deputies. Why didn't you go yourself?"

"I was busy. They were minor charges, anyway. Spotlighting, illegal fishing. I didn't expect any trouble . . . not killing, anyway."

"You knew Crawford and Anderson were at daggers' points."

"Because of Anderson's wife? So what? I deputized Crawford. Besides, he asked for the job. He was looking forward to making Anderson squirm."

"Anderson squirmed kind of rough, didn't he?" Garth said, acid in his tone.

"That's enough out of you, Garth," Uhle said coldly. "Take your car and go back the way you came."

"Think you'll ever get Anderson?" Garth taunted. "It's ten days now."

"We've got him right here, within a two-mile area. He spent last night in the old lodge. We found a raincoat he abandoned and a half-full bottle of whiskey and some crackers. He must have heard us coming and beat it fast. But we've got him penned in. We'll get him. Don't worry."

"Dead or alive?"

Uhle's grin was animal in quality, a mirthless lifting of his upper lip from his teeth. "You know what Anderson said. He'll never let himself be taken alive. Frankly, that suits me fine."

Distaste ran strong in Garth. "You're mighty brave," he said with contempt, "when you've got two hundred men at your back. I read all about you in the papers. How you said you'd get Roy dead or alive. Leonard Uhle. The scourge of the lawless."

Uhle lifted the submachine gun he was holding. He reversed it with the butt end pointing at Garth. "I ought to ram your teeth down your throat. You sound off just once more, Garth, and so help me, that's exactly what I'll do."

"Will you be that brave when you meet Anderson? If there's just the two of you?"

"One last chance, Garth. Beat it. Quick. You stay here one minute longer, and I'm putting irons on you and having you hauled off to the jug."

Garth could see that this was the end of talk, the end of bluff. "All right, Uhle," he said quietly. "I'll go." He walked around his car and got in. Through the open window he said: "See you around."

He turned the car and drove off. Until he was out of sight, he could feel Uhle's glance on him, hard and angry and implacable.

Before he reached the roadblock, he found a seldom-used fire lane and turned off where the highway forked. Once the lane had been a logging railroad. The rails had been torn up along with the ties, and the roadbed had been graded to make it passable for cars. Tall, wild grass grew between the ruts made by the few vehicles that still traveled the lane. He could hear the rustling sound the grass made against the bottom of the car.

Some of the way he had to proceed in second gear. Even so, the car bumped and bounced over the rough spots. It splashed through stagnant puddles of water, and once he felt the car slow and begin to drag as though something had clutched it and was reluctant to let go. He gunned the engine, splattering dirty water and mire, and at the last instant felt the tires grab. With a lurch the car jerked out of the mud hole and rolled freely again.

The fire lane curved through some slashings, a large clearing where, years ago, fire had swept through the cutover land, burning the piles of trimmed branches and tops. Now there was just the vast emptiness and desolation, the wild grass and weeds, waving tall in the warm wind, and here and there the stripped, charred trunk of a tree, a lonely, solitary reminder of the fury of the flames. Then the trees closed in on either side of the road, so close in places that branches scratched loudly against the sides of the car and every now and then made him wince and flinch against his will when they struck the windshield.

After a while, the forest withdrew a little, and branches no longer scraped. Through the open window of the car he could hear the running of a river, and then the road made a sharp curve, and he pulled off to the side where the fire lane branched off into an old gravel pit.

He got his rifle and stepped out. The river ran nearby, whispering its ancient, cryptic secrets. All about the forest hovered, serene and patient and inestimably lonely. The sky was yellow with haze, and the sun beat down with scorching intensity.

He slapped at a mosquito that had punctured the skin of his bare forearm, and a spot of blood showed where the insect had fed. He waved a gnat away, the sweat running slowly, stickily down his chest and back.

He took a few steps toward the river, his head bowed in thought. *Jill,* he was thinking, *you don't know how impossible it is. Miles of wilderness. I could pass right next to him without noticing him. He'd have to move, or make some sign. The only way I can find him is for him to come to me. I wouldn't be doing this for anyone else, only for you, Jill.*

He spotted the deer tracks on some hard clay and followed them with his eyes. He looked without much interest, until on the far side of the pit, near the timber's edge, he spied a small pool of blood.

His muscles tensed, and he could feel his heart race as he followed the tracks. At the forest's edge he paused, prudence and caution warning him not to proceed further. The forest stared at him with a thousand hidden eyes, challenging him, mocking him. He felt the first flickerings of fear, tremulous quaverings in his muscles, but he closed his mind to them. Drawing a deep breath, he parted some brush and stepped into the timber.

Drops of blood on a hazel bush, a splotch of blood on the bole of a white birch, a tiny carmine pool on the damp floor of the forest guided him. And he had the tracks, also, to show him the way, sharp imprints on the wet earth. A mosquito bit him on the back of the neck and another on the wrist. Sweat trickled with oily stickiness down his body.

The doe lay dead beside a windfall. Garth stood and stared down. The doe had been shot, but death had not come to her from a bullet. Death had come from the knife that had slashed her throat.

His eyes searched the forest, but all they saw were the silent trees and the gloom dotted here and there with tiny patches of light where the sun managed to filter through. All at once the forest became a living thing, waiting with breathless patience, waiting to pounce, to destroy. Sounds, magnified by apprehension, reached his ears. The snapping of a twig? But twigs never snapped that loud. Something crawling in the brush? But stalking beasts moved much quicker than that. His heart was a drum, beating an urgent alarm.

"Hold it, Garth."

He leapt backward so violently that the rifle almost dropped from his fingers. For an instant he remained white-lipped, motionless, staring into the shadows. Then he had himself in hand.

"Don't try anything," a familiar voice warned. "Put your rifle down on the windfall. Then move away from it."

His boots made soft, sucking noises on the moist earth as he complied. He wanted to turn, to try to see, but he did not dare. The voice was not loud; it was not even angry. It was just cool and indifferent, like an executioner's axe.

Anderson sat on the windfall with Garth's rifle leaning against the old fallen tree and his own rifle across his knees. He scratched absently at a mosquito bite on his chest. Ten days' growth of whiskers matted his face. He smelled of sweat and spruce needles and resin.

"How many with you, Garth?"

"I'm alone."

"You sure?"

"Positive."

Anderson glanced along the way Garth had come. Anderson's blue eyes were sharp. He had the keen senses of the hunted. His head cocked slightly to one side in an attitude of concentrated listening. After a while, his glance returned to Garth.

"How come?"

Garth shrugged. He made no answer.

Anderson sighed, a soft, melancholy sound. "I really don't much care. Do you understand, Garth? I don't care if you're not alone."

Garth said nothing.

Blue eyes studied Garth. There was nothing in them but weariness. "What brings you here?" Anderson asked. "I never did anything to you."

Garth did not speak.

"I've never liked you," Anderson said, "because you went with Jill before I married her. I know you don't like me. But neither one of us ever did anything to the other." A faint, wry smile touched Anderson's mouth briefly. "Is it the mob fever, Garth? How many men do they have hunting me, anyway?"

"They figure around two hundred."

The smile returned for a fleeting moment. It was sad and tired now. "Is that right? I didn't think I was that important."

"You killed two men."

The blue eyes blazed. The weariness fled; the face grew hard and relentless in an instant. "And I'd kill Crawford all over again. I wish I could kill him a thousand times, each time a little more painful than the one before. I killed him too quick. I should've stretched it out as long as I could."

The wrath abruptly vanished, and Anderson's shoulders slumped. "I'm sorry about Charlie Erdman, though. I never meant to kill Charlie . . . just Crawford."

"How come you shot Erdman, then?" Garth asked.

"I didn't expect Charlie. I was out at my shack. Uhle came first, but I told that blundering, ugly son-of-a-bitch off. I took his gun away from him and slapped him around and told him to send Crawford to get me. I knew it was Crawford behind the charges. He wanted me out of the way."

Anderson's chest swelled as he drew a breath and held it. When he exhaled, it was with a lingering, audible sound. "Well, Crawford came, with Erdman. I saw them. So I got my rifle and waited. Someone pounded on the door, and Crawford hollered for me to open up. I told him to come in. When the door opened, I fired. But instead of Crawford, it was poor Charlie. Crawford ran, but I got him. I'm sorry for Charlie."

"That doesn't help him any," Garth said.

"No. I don't think it does." For a moment Anderson's

eyes looked agonized. Then they turned tired again. "Did Jill send you?" His tone was very quiet now, like the weary wind striving to reveal secrets that no one can understand.

Garth nodded.

"It figures," Anderson said. "Why?"

"She wants you to give up."

Anderson laughed. It was an almost silent laugh — low, brittle, without mirth. "Why?" he asked.

"She said, if you die, she'll blame herself for it the rest of her life. She's already blaming herself for Crawford and Erdman."

"You want to know something, Garth? I don't give a damn *what* she feels."

Garth looked away, at the doe lying dead and still with flies buzzing around the drying blood, and then at the calm, indifferent face of the forest. He could not find anything to say.

"Did she tell you anything?" Anderson's voice sounded choked.

Garth spoke with reluctance. "Enough," he said quietly.

"About Crawford?"

"Are you sure it was Crawford?"

"I wouldn't have killed him, if I wasn't sure." Anderson paused. He appeared to be thinking of something. "You know what I am," he said slowly. "You know what I've always been. Sometimes I think I was born out of my time. I'm not for the city, a home in town. I've hunted and trapped, mostly violated . . . spotlighting deer, dynamiting and netting fish. Oh, there's a little money in that, if you have the right connections, and I had them. I got the venison and the fish, and Crawford delivered them. Uhle, too, before he got to be sheriff."

He saw the look on Garth's face and laughed softly, with

bitter mirth. "Yes, Len Uhle. After he got to be sheriff, he took his rake-offs for leaving us alone. It's not a pretty picture, is it?"

Garth said nothing. He stood and stared into darkness.

"It was Crawford, all right," Anderson went on, his voice bleak with brooding. "I came home one night in time to see a man leave. He was big and husky, like Crawford, and then Crawford sounded off all over town. I hadn't paid any attention before then because he was always bragging about the women he'd slept with or could sleep with. Mostly it was only talk. But after I saw . . . it was Crawford, all right."

"I can't believe it of her," Garth said.

"I found it hard to believe, too," Anderson said. "You went with her. You must have liked her an awful lot. But I married her. She was my wife. If I hadn't loved her, I'd have killed her, too."

"He could have forced her. He could have said he'd make trouble for you, if she didn't give in."

Anderson shrugged. "What's the difference? It's been done. I'm all dead inside, Garth. I have no feeling for her any more."

Garth stared hard at Anderson. But the man had his glance on something far away, something only he could see. "You're serious about not surrendering?" Garth asked.

It was a full minute before Anderson came back to the present. "I'm not trying to get out of taking my medicine," he said. "I got a lot coming for killing Charlie Erdman, even for killing that rat, Crawford. But this state doesn't have a death penalty . . . only life imprisonment."

He scraped dirt with the toe of a boot. "It would be hell for me in prison. I couldn't even stand it in a small town. The woods . . . that's where my life is . . . that's where my death will be."

He rose and picked up Garth's rifle and tossed it at the man. Surprise was so great in Garth that he barely managed to catch the gun. Anderson smiled.

"I'm going now, Garth. Shoot me if you like. I've had a lot of time to think these past ten days. I finally know what I want." He glanced at the dead doe. "I took a chance and shot that deer because I was hungry. I was going to break into some place after dark and cook some of it. Now I won't even take any with me."

He said no word of farewell. He turned and a few strides later was gone from sight in the tangle of brush and timber. A few sounds came back, growing ever fainter. Then there was the silence, the vast, knowing silence of the forest.

Garth thought he had lost the trail until he came to the road, and there in the dust he saw the tracks, crossing the road and disappearing into the timber again. *He means it,* he thought, while something sad and pitying stirred in him. *He means it about dying. He's headed right for them, right for Uhle.*

He wanted to break into a run, but then it came to him that the matter was out of his hands. It lay now with destiny.

He climbed a slope and down the other side, where the trees had been thinned out by man. Spruces and balsams grew here, spaced neatly apart, and sod covered the earth and grass that had been mowed. Through the avenues in the trees he could see the sparkling blue of a lake ahead.

As he reached the rim of the trees, he heard the shouts, and then he saw Anderson. The man ran with a strange, careless lope. He reached the shore of the lake and began to fiddle with the ropes mooring a boat to a pier. The ropes seemed to give him trouble for it was taking him a long time. The shouting broke out again, and Anderson straightened and raised the rifle.

The volley broke like thunder. Anderson went stumbling back. At the water's edge his knees buckled. The chatter of a submachine gun sounded, and the rifle dropped from Anderson's hands, and he folded over gently on his side, like a tired man laying himself down to rest.

"I said I'd get him!" Uhle was shouting as Garth walked up. "I said I wouldn't give up until I had him, dead or alive. Ten days it took, but I got him."

He strutted back and forth on the beach in front of the dead man. Water lapped gently at Anderson's boots. "You heard me. All you men are witnesses. You heard me shout to him to stop. He turned instead. He was going to shoot. That's when I let him have it. He asked for it, and by damn he got it. All you men are witnesses."

Why so loud, Uhle? Garth thought, while something grim and frightening moved in him, a knowledge that he should have been aware of long before now. *Why so much? You sound happy, like things turned out just like you wanted them to.*

Uhle spotted Garth. "You! What the hell you doing back here? Where'd you come from?"

Garth jerked his head at the forest. "The same way Anderson came."

"Anderson?" Uhle looked startled. "You were in the woods with Anderson? What did you do?"

"Talked to him."

"About what?"

"Many things, Uhle. Just about everything, in fact."

"Why the hell didn't you arrest him?"

"You wouldn't deputize me. Remember? And then, I wouldn't want to take any glory away from you."

"Don't needle me, Garth."

"I can wait," Garth said quietly.

"Wait for what?"

"You figure that out," Garth said, his eyes hard and steady. "I'll give you enough time to figure it out. If you don't catch on, then I'll tell you."

Uhle tried to meet Garth's stare, but Uhle's eyes would not hold. They sidled off to the waiting, watchful men. "I've had enough of your silly riddles. You and me are having this out when I get back to town. Right now, I've got other things to do. Pete, you and a couple of the boys stay here. I'll send the coroner out soon as I get to town."

He started away. Garth worked the lever of his .30-30, quick and hard. The sound was sharp and loud. Uhle flinched and spun around, eyes for an instant wild and full of panic. Garth grinned and looked down at the ejected shell, his fingers still tightly on the lever.

"What the hell are you doing, Garth?"

"Unloading my rifle."

Uhle's mouth opened to speak, but then he thought better of it. He moved off without another word.

It's over for Anderson, Garth was thinking as he watched Uhle's back, *but for you it's just beginning. It wasn't Crawford. It was you, Uhle. That's why you wanted Anderson dead so bad. So he wouldn't catch on. But I've caught on, and I'll make Jill tell me. You so much as bother her just once and that will be enough for me. I'll probably kill you one of these days. So think and sweat, Uhle. Think and sweat and wonder. You'll never know when it's going to happen.*

Uhle got in his car and started it. Garth watched until it was out of sight. And in him the darkness and cruel purpose kept growing.

The Happy Death

"It is not good to die sad or alone," the *viejo* said. "Summon them, Teresina, my family, that I may have them all about me as I leave this mortal life."

"We are going to have to suffer through that again?" Teresina asked in a tone of disgust. "This is the fifth time in a year that you have announced you are about to die."

The old man coughed, and then shifted his position on the blankets to avoid the dripping from the new leak in the roof. The winter rain was a soft patter on the old house. Outside, the California day was gray with mist and gloom.

"How you abuse me." Moisture filmed the *viejo*'s eyes, his white *mustachios* quivered. "You who are the wife of my only son, to whom I have always been most kind and generous and. . . ."

"Hah! You have been a drunkard and a thief and a nuisance. It is you who abuses me." She stopped stirring the kettle of beans and dipped out a spoonful to taste. Several beans spilled to the floor, and Juanito, the youngest, who still crawled, made his way to them and one by one stuffed them in his mouth with gusto. Seeing this, Teresina carefully dropped several more beans on the floor. "You are not going to die. You will outlive us all."

"How you mock me." The *viejo* shifted position quickly to avoid a sudden rill of raindrops. "Is it much that I ask? That my family be summoned? Will you go fetch them for me, Dulces? Be a good. . . ."

"Are you insane?" Teresina twitched her hefty shoulders

angrily. "Dulces has but two years, and it is raining without."

"Ampara?" the *viejo* asked beseechingly.

Ampara sat in a far corner, reading. She did not lift her eyes.

Teresina made a low, tired sound. "Always with the magazines of the moving pictures. She has time for nothing else. Such a daughter I have raised."

"Pepe?" the *viejo* asked.

"He is with Román over to the *Señor* McManus. There is a truck that must be repaired of the brakes. The *Señor* McManus declares that Pepe is very skillful in the repairing and adjusting of the brakes."

"And Doroteo and Alfredo?"

Teresina emitted a sound of surrender. "You will not give up, will you, *obstinado?*" She waddled over to the door and stuck her head out. "Alfredo! Doroteo! Fetch your father and Pepe! For your grandfather. The usual."

From the creek, where they were fishing, came the boys' faint shouts. "Hooray! Grandpapa is dying again. We will go instantly."

Teresina turned and waddled back to the stove. The *viejo* lay back on the blankets and closed his eyes and sighed happily.

The *viejo*'s eyes brimmed with tears. Great emotions clashed within his breast. "It is so good . . . it is so fine," he said, "to see all my family here about me. So good of you to come also, *Señor* Jeem. You provide my Román with a job, his wife and little ones with a home. I shall smile down upon you every day from heaven."

Carefully, with trembling fingers, the *viejo* opened the cigar box which he had beside him. "My dearest possessions. My worldly goods. For you first, Juanito. This ring. From my grandfather and his grandfather before him, I give. . . ."

"From the store of the ten cents," Teresina interrupted. "Fool. He will swallow it. Give it here, at once."

"As you wish, dear Teresina. For you, Dulces, this lovely brooch, from my grandmother and her grandmother, a gift from the governor of. . . ."

"Also from the store of the ten cents," Teresina broke in again. "Hand it here or she will pinch herself."

The *viejo* sighed. "Alfredo, Doroteo. For each of you a *cuchillo,* a knife from the days when I rode with Villa, as a sergeant. I carried them in the battle of. . . ."

"The last time you died, Grandpapa," Alfredo said, "you were a corporal."

"I am old," the *viejo* said. "I grow confused. Once I was a corporal, true, but then I was promoted to sergeant, for saving Villa's life at Columbus. I. . . ."

"Was it not at Guererro that you saved his life?" Pepe asked.

"At both places, Pepe. My eldest grandson. The image of your father. This sash. From the presidential palace in *Ciudad Mejíco* when I was Villa's lieutenant."

"Was it not the palace of the governor of Chihuahua?" Pepe asked.

"I grow faint. Memory dims," the *viejo* said. "Do not mock your grandpapa. My time is short. Ampara."

Teresina had to shout the name before the girl stirred, and then put her magazine aside and came over slowly, sullenly, to where the family was grouped about the old man. She had the early ripeness and roundness of Mexican girls, and dark, liquid eyes and full, red lips.

"Ampara. This string of pearls. It is said they graced the

throat of Carlotta when Mexico had an Empress. I. . . ."

"They give away better in boxes of crackerjack," Ampara said boredly.

The *viejo*'s eyes brimmed. "So be it. The last of my worldly possessions. To you, Román, my son, and to you, dear Teresina, I can give only my blessing."

"You will be all right, Papa," Román said, caressing the *viejo*'s hand. He turned to McManus. "The rain, the cold, the gloom of the days. They always affect him thus."

"Maybe he needs a doctor," McManus said. "Maybe medicine."

"He will be all right," Román said.

The *viejo* coughed and cleared his throat. "It is said that a little wine, boiled, is good for certain disturbances of the blood. Just a few spoonfuls. Heated."

McManus grinned, but the *viejo* — whose glance was still sharp — noted that the humor did not reach McManus's eyes. "If you'll send Pepe back with me, Román, I'll give him a gallon. I've got more wine than I can use."

"You are so kind, *Señor* Jeem," the *viejo* said. "I, Eladio Garza, would like very much to repay you. Is there not something I can do?"

A shadow darkened and hardened McManus's face. The gray eyes looked into the distance. "Thank you, Eladio, but I need nothing." He rose and, accompanied by Pepe, left the room.

Rain pattered on the roof. Juanito began to squall, and then Dulces followed his example. Ampara wandered back to her magazine. Doroteo and Alfredo began tossing the knives at the wall. Román hunkered on his heels and stared at the *viejo*.

"He is a good man, the *Señor* Jeem," the old man said.

"Do you, perchance, know of what troubles him, Román?"

"There is one who comes to the ranch now and then. *Un malo hombre* . . . a wicked man, for he brings nothing but unhappiness to the *Señor* McManus. After every visit, the *Señor* McManus grows sad and grim. He and his wife do not smile. They sit with long faces."

The *viejo*'s eyes narrowed. "Have you no idea why these visits should desolate the *Señor* Jeem as they do?"

Román spread his hands. "Who knows? An old enmity? A feud of the blood."

Ampara looked up from her magazine, eyes shining excitedly. "It is perhaps like that which I saw once in the motion pictures. There is this man who knows some evil secret about the hero and demands much money to remain silent and so. . . ."

"It is well for *you* to remain silent," the *viejo* reprimanded. "Also, Ampara, this is talk for your elders."

Ampara pouted and returned to her reading.

"Is there no other reason you can think of?" the *viejo* asked Román.

Román shook his head.

For a long while the *viejo* stared up at the ceiling, while thoughts sped through his mind. Then something roused him and brought him up on an elbow.

"Hark. Is that Pepe? With my wine? Such a good boy. When I am in heaven, I shall smile down upon him every day."

The morning sun could not be seen through the mist that hovered overhead. The drenched earth steamed. The creek which flowed not far from the house was swollen and noisy with the rushing accumulation of the week-long rain.

The *viejo* sat on the stoop with a fruit jar half full of wine beside him and watched Jim McManus cross the bridge over the creek which was all but overflowing its banks. McManus grinned and waved a hand when he spied the *viejo,* but the *viejo* noted that the worry still lurked on McManus's face.

Dark wrinkles lay under the eyes as though McManus had not slept the night before. Compassion filled the *viejo.*

"How goes it, Eladio?" McManus said. "Did the wine do you well?"

"The blood of a youth surges in my veins this morning," the *viejo* said, "but the legs are still those of an old man. *Gracias, Señor* Jeem, for the kindness of the wine. If I could but repay you. . . . I grieve."

McManus stared down at the *viejo.* "There is no need, Eladio. We are *amigos.* What are *amigos* for, if not to do kindness without pay?"

"True," the *viejo* said, nodding. "Still, I would like to repay, if there were some way."

McManus clapped the *viejo* on the shoulder. "Do not trouble yourself with such thoughts, Eladio. Your friendship is payment enough for me." He started off.

The *viejo* watched McManus go. Then the old man shifted to a spot on the stoop that seemed warmer. Dulces toddled around the house and took a drink of the wine. Teresina, from the door, saw. Her voice brimmed with righteous anger.

"*Borrachón* . . . is it not enough that you set a bad example? Must you also make my precious little Dulces into a drunkard like yourself?"

The *viejo* shook the fruit jar. "It is empty," he said sadly. "Fetch me another, please, Teresina?"

"Fetch it yourself," Teresina snapped, and turned back inside the house. From within, her voice came, a steady, irate murmur itemizing all her burdens and complaints.

Ampara appeared in the doorway, then sat down beside the *viejo.* "It is truly bad, Grandpapa, about the *Señor* McManus?"

The *viejo* sighed. "I fear it is. I have been thinking. It must be as you said last night, a matter of paying much money to the *malo hombre*."

Ampara's eyes widened. "What do you think will happen? Will he lose his ranch and we our home?"

"There is the possibility."

"Is there not anything at all that can be done?"

"If the good Lord were to send a lightning bolt to strike the *malo hombre,* if the earth were to open and swallow him, if . . . what approaches, Ampara? My eyes this morning are full of sun."

Ampara giggled. "More full of wine, you mean." She sobered under the *viejo*'s stern, indignant look. "It is a car." She jumped to her feet. "Such a car."

The car — a gleaming red and white sedan — came down the hill and stopped on the far side of the creek. A man got out and walked ahead to examine the rickety bridge. After a while, he began to walk across. Boards creaked and trembled. Churning water rushed underneath. The stranger came on toward the *viejo* and Ampara, flashing a gold-toothed grin.

"That bridge won't support much more than my weight," the stranger said. He gazed with frank admiration at Ampara. The *viejo* belched, groaned, and placed a hand beneath his heart. "What's the matter with him?" the stranger asked.

"I am dying," the *viejo* said.

"He dies quite regularly," Ampara explained. "This is the fifth instance this year. Pay no attention to him. The time to worry is when he is not dying."

"Oh," the stranger said, but the look on his pink, heavy face was puzzled. He brightened as he turned his eyes back on Ampara.

The *viejo* sat up quite straight. "I did not catch your name, *señor*."

"Sam Butler."

The *viejo* nodded politely. "I would rise and shake hands, *Señor* Butler, but, as you can see, I am dying."

The stranger turned to Ampara. "Look, honey, is McManus around?"

Ampara looked at the *viejo* who turned his eyes heavenward and shrugged. "*Sí,*" Ampara said. "Up on the hill. Mending the fence. See?"

The stranger looked to where Ampara pointed. His hand dropped with exaggerated casualness on her hip. "Thanks a lot, honey. See you later maybe, huh?"

Ampara giggled. The stranger left. The *viejo* sighed his weary sigh. "That *Señor* Butler. A bad one. Poor *Señor* Jeem. My heart bleeds. I grieve."

The *viejo* lay back against the stoop with his eyes closed. The white *mustachios* quivered each time he exhaled. The fruit jar, emptied again, lay toppled on its side. But the *viejo* was not sleeping. He heard footsteps approaching, pause as someone stared down at him, then their moving on.

When all was silence except for the squalling of Juanito within the house, the *viejo* stirred and sat up and studiously observed the tableau on the far side of the creek. Leaning against a crimson fender of the sedan was Ampara and close, very close, to her was the stranger.

The *viejo* could not hear what was being said, but Ampara giggled and laughed often. Now and then the stranger put a hand on her, but Ampara expertly swayed and curved out from under it and then as skillfully swayed back within reach again. The *viejo* watched, his face a mask, and once nodded faintly. Then his eyes began to droop. Dulces came and tipped the fruit jar to her mouth and whimpered at its emptiness.

The sound of a starting motor brought the *viejo*'s eyes open once again. The car had difficulty turning around in the narrow confines between the bottom of the slope and the creek. The ground was wet, and the tires slipped and spun. The *viejo* held his breath, waiting for the car to roll into the water, but the stranger got out of his difficulty and finally started back up the hill.

Ampara returned, walking proudly. "He has made a date with me, Grandpapa. He is to come for me tonight."

The *viejo* grunted.

"Are you not going to say anything?"

"Go to the house of the *Señor* Jeem and fetch more wine."

"Is that all you can say?"

"Fetch the wine. *¡Pronto!*" There was anger in the *viejo*'s tone, the hint that he would tolerate no disobedience. Ampara shrugged and started for the bridge.

Ampara wore her good dress, the red one she had washed and pressed that day. The *viejo* thought the bright color went very well with the darkness of Ampara's hair and eyes. He knew pride as he stared at her, for she was his granddaughter. Like Delores del Rio, he thought, remembering the only motion picture he had ever seen.

He sat at the table with Román who stared into nothingness. There had been a great quarrel that morning between the stranger and McManus, and afterward McManus had been most upset. So Román drank now and then from his fruit jar and brooded.

The boys — Pepe, Doroteo, and Alfredo — were outside, playing at throwing rocks at one another. An occasional stone struck the house, and once one came through the glassless window. Juanito crawled over and put the stone in his mouth. Dulces kept tugging at the *viejo*'s trousers, wanting wine, but Teresina's baleful glance kept darting to the old one, and he did not dare please Dulces.

He saw that Román's jar was empty, so he filled it anew. Román lifted it and all but drained it. He belched, and juice of the grape trickled out of the corners of his mouth. His eyes turned strangely luminescent. The viejo watched him carefully.

"To battle!" Román's voice was a roar that caused Dulces to squeal and Juanito to choke on the stone in his mouth. While Teresina upended Juanito and pounded his back, Román lurched to his feet. "To the wars!" he shouted, brandishing a fist. "I fear no one, neither the armies of this world nor those of the outer planets. Is there no one to battle me?" His chair crashed over as he stumbled away from the table. "*¡Cobardes!* Who will give me battle?" Abruptly he collapsed and lay sprawled on the floor, snoring.

The *viejo* sighed. "Poor Román. He never could take much wine."

At that moment there came the loud blast of a car horn from beyond the creek. "It is he, it is he!" Ampara cried excitedly, and gave her dress one last smoothing.

"Ampara," the *viejo* said sternly as the girl started for the door, "remember your manners. You must invite the *Señor* Butler within. Politeness and courtesy demand it."

Ampara was soon back, holding onto the arm of the stranger.

"Enter, enter," the *viejo* cried, rising to his feet. "*Señor* Butler, my home is yours. Teresina. A glass for the *Señor* Butler. Quick. Quick. A glass."

They possessed only the one good glass and had saved it for the stranger. Teresina placed it carefully on the table, and the *viejo* poured it full. Under Ampara's urging, the stranger wended his way between Juanito and Dulces. On the floor, Román snored a steady rhythm.

"Sit," the *viejo* said. "Drink. I would have you as my guest a while." He cocked an ear, listening to the shouts of the boys outside. He could hear Alfredo and Doroteo, but not Pepe. The *viejo* nodded to himself. *Good,* he thought, *it starts well.* "Drink," he urged the stranger who seemed somewhat ill at ease. And when the glass had been drained, the *viejo* said: "Ampara, fill his glass again."

The stranger glanced at Ampara who smiled and nestled up to him. "Let's go, baby," he said. "I got no time for creeps."

"*Señor* Butler, pardon," the *viejo* said. "Why such a hurry?" I wish to make talk with you."

The stranger looked at his watch. "The drive-in is open. The picture's gonna start any minute now. You don't want me to miss any of it, do you, honey?"

The *viejo* looked stern. "*Señor* Butler. Pardon. I wish to know something about you. Ampara is my granddaughter. I feel a great responsibility for her. Although she has sixteen years, she is innocent, and it is my wish that she remain so. Therefore, I demand to know something of you before I allow her to leave in your company."

The stranger spoke, telling of his life. The *viejo* nodded approvingly throughout the recitation, filling the wine glass and his fruit jar each time they emptied. When the stranger was through, the *viejo* insisted on narrating his military experiences as a revolutionary under Pancho Villa in old Mexico. When the *viejo* finished, the wine gallon was all but empty. The *viejo* rose, weaving on his feet.

"You satisfy me, *Señor* Butler. I entrust my Ampara to your care. I know you will treat her like a true gentleman."

Afterward the *viejo* explained to McManus: "Such a tragedy. My face is made white by it. When the *Señor* Butler went to turn his car, the brakes would not hold, and the car plunged into the creek, drowning the *Señor* Butler who could not get out. Fortunately, my Ampara was not within the car. She had remained without to guide the *Señor* Butler while he turned it." The *viejo* shook his head and clucked his tongue. "It is true, what they say, that he who drinks should not take upon himself the driving of a car."

McManus stared hard at the *viejo.* "Is what you have told me the truth?"

The *viejo* waved a hand. "Perhaps I have concealed a little. Pepe, he is skillful in the repairing and adjusting of the brakes, is he not? He will be a great mechanic some day, that one. While I entertained the *Señor* Butler, Pepe proceeded to drain the fluid of the brakes. Who is there to say that the fluid did not drain of itself?"

McManus stared long and hard at the *viejo.* He tried, but he could not speak.

"Why mourn?" the *viejo* asked. "He died full of wine and in joyful spirits. What death could be happier?" He lay back on his blankets and coughed and groaned. "It is not good to die sad or alone. Teresina, summon my family that I may have them all about me as I leave this mortal life once and for all."

Bad Blood

Me and Cal rode into Río Seco about ten by the sun. The minute we hit town, I could feel the hate in the air. As we passed the O. K. Livery, a pebble came flying out of the wide door, hitting Cal's orange dun on the rump. The dun shied and started to rear, and Cal had to rein him in hard. Cal stared to swear.

"Blame' kid," he said. "I'll fix him."

"Let it be," I told Cal.

"I just want to give him a good swift boot."

"Let it ride."

"Hang it, Joe, he threw a rock at me."

"As long as it's only rocks . . . ," I said.

We rode on. In front of Lew Forrest's saloon we pulled over to the hitching rack and stepped down and tied our horses. Cal was grumbling under his breath. He stretched and shoved his hat to the back of his head and with his hand swept some of the sweat from his face.

"I don't know what the devil's the matter with Río Seco, Joe. We're the law here in Cinco County, but not even a couple of blacklegs would get treated as bad as us. What the hell's the matter with everyone, anyway?"

"You know what's the matter."

I started for Forrest's door, but Cal said: "Joe."

I stopped. "Yes?"

"Look, it's all over now. It's three months over. Why not drop it?"

"Is it over?"

Cal was sweating hard. It was very hot here in Río Seco today. "You can't change anything, Joe. It's too late for that."

"Maybe I can't change anything, but I've got to know for sure." I looked him in the eyes. "You can ride back to Fort Benson. I told you I could handle this myself."

He began kicking at the ground with a toe. "You know I'll back you. I've backed you all my life. It's just that I can't see any good coming of this."

"I'm the sheriff, Cal. I'll decide what this office is going to do."

Lew Forrest had only one customer, one of Frank Tollison's Spanish Bit cowboys named Johnny Rayburn. He had come into town for the mail. It was there on the bar beside him. I bought Johnny a drink because me and Cal had worked for Spanish Bit before I had run for sheriff.

I had a sip of beer, and then I said: "You see much of Ed Miller these days, Lew?"

Lew shrugged and made a pass at the bar with a damp towel. "No more, no less, than usual."

"When you see him last?"

"Oh. Three, four days maybe."

"That long?"

Lew grinned. "He does a lot of drinking at home now. Comes in and stocks up and I don't see him for a week sometimes. Guess it saves him a lot of wear and tear this way from not falling off a horse so much."

I looked at Cal. He was staring down into his beer like he wasn't much interested in what was going on. I looked back at Lew Forrest. "Ed owe you anything?" I asked.

Lew started wiping the bar even though it didn't need it. He didn't answer me.

"Did you hear me, Lew?" I said.

He went on wiping the same spot on the bar. "I heard you."

"Well?"

"Look, I don't see where it's any of your business who owes me what, even if you are sheriff."

"I think maybe in this case it might be my business."

"Just what are you driving at?"

"Ed doesn't work anywhere," I told him. "He's let his ranch go to pot. Yet I hear he's been drinking pretty heavy lately. No one gives away whiskey for free, Lew."

He made two more passes at the bar, then gave it up. "I don't like to make trouble for no one. I can't afford to in my business. I don't like to cause Ed no trouble. He's a good customer of mine."

"How good?"

Lew shrugged. He said nothing.

"Don't go against me. I'll remember it, if you do."

"I don't ask my customers where they get their money. They come in and spend it and that's that. You can't hold me responsible for how they get it."

"That's not what I'm talking about. What I want to know is . . . does Ed Miller pay you for the liquor he drinks?"

"Do you think I'd give him any, if he didn't?"

"It took you long enough to say so," I told him. I finished my beer and ordered another round.

This softened him up. He served the beers, and then he leaned across the bar and dropped his voice, but not enough so that Cal and even Johnny couldn't hear. "I don't want to cause nobody trouble. I can't afford to. But I always did think it was funny about Ed. He not only pays me for what he drinks, but he also squared up an old bill. I always wondered where he got the money, but that's none of my business. You understand that, don't you?"

I didn't bother to answer him. I told Cal to drink up.

"What you figure him for, Joe?" Lew asked. "Rustling, maybe?"

"Maybe I don't figure him for anything," I told Lew, and started for the door.

I paused by the hitching rack, trying to decide what to do next. Cal came out and stood there, sweating in the sun. I saw him glance up the street and the change that came over his face, and I looked that way, too, and saw her.

She had come out of the Mercantile with a couple of bundles in her arms, and her way was taking her past us. She didn't notice us until it was too late, or she'd have crossed the street. Her chin went up, and the ring of her heels on the boardwalk became loud and clear.

I nodded and touched my hat to her as she went by. Cal tipped his Stetson and said: "Howdy, Miss Ada."

She passed us like we weren't there.

Cal followed her with his eyes until she was gone from sight. Then he said: "She doesn't even look at me any more."

I didn't say anything. There really was nothing to say. The words had died at the end of a noose three months ago.

I told Cal to wait for me there at Lew Forrest's, and then I cut across town to where Ada Sears lived. I rapped on the door, and I heard her heels coming, but, when she saw me through the screen, she stopped. A moment later, however, she came the rest of the way.

"Why don't you go away?" she said. "You know you're not welcome here."

"I'd like to talk to you, Miss Ada."

"There's nothing for us to talk about."

"I think there is."

"You should have talked to me three months ago. You

should have believed me then."

"I had nothing to do with the believing or the judging. That was out of my hands."

"I know," she said. "All you do is the hanging."

It was like she had stuck a knife in me and twisted it. I couldn't find anything to say.

"Go away," she said. "Don't ever come here again."

She started to go, and I said: "Miss Ada . . . wait."

I thought she wouldn't, but she stopped and looked back at me over her shoulder.

"You knew him. Did he have any enemies?"

She came back now with her head thrust forward, and she hurled the words at me. "Lots of them. Oh, he had lots of enemies."

"Who?"

"You, Joe, and Cal Winter and Frank Tollison and all of Spanish Bit and Judge Fitzpatrick and Ben Arnette. The bunch of you killed him."

"Please, Miss Ada. Don't talk like that. I don't care what you say about me or the others, but don't talk like that about Cal. He doesn't deserve it."

"He brought Roy in, didn't he?"

"He had to. Ed Miller reported it to Cal, and he had to pick Roy up."

"Nothing will ever change the way I feel," she said.

I could see how useless it was, but, as long as I had started it, I thought I'd carry on. "Won't you try to go along with me? Won't you tell me what I want to know?"

"Now that he's dead, you're beginning to think he might have been innocent. Why didn't you think so while he was alive?"

I couldn't find anything to say to this.

"If you find the guilty one," she said, "what will you do?"

"He'll pay. He'll pay good."

"Will that bring Roy back to me?" She started to cry now, very softly. "That's all you men ever think about in this country, killing and hanging. For nothing at all you'll kill and hang. Why don't you go away and leave me alone?"

She turned again, and this time I let her go. After a while I started back to Lew Forrest's. The sound of her crying stayed in my ears all the way.

Cal was inside the saloon, drinking whiskey now. I gave him a hard look, and his eyes shifted to a point beyond me.

"I just had a couple," he said.

"That doesn't help any," I told him. "You've tried it before, and you know it doesn't help."

"But it was only two, this time."

"Was it?" I said. "Let's go."

We got our horses and rode out of Río Seco, out into the heat and the sun, and it seemed that some of the hate in the air went along with us. We crossed the wooden bridge over the dry creekbed and turned northward to where the crests of the Capitáns showed, shimmering through the heat waves.

Cal rode for a while with his head bowed like he was thinking on something and finally he said: "I don't know why she acts the way she does. Do you, Joe?"

I knew, but I wasn't telling him because he knew, too, no matter what he said.

"I know she loved him," Cal went on, "and they were going to be married, but what happened wasn't my fault. He's butchering Spanish Bit cattle, and Billy Vesper catches him at it, and so he kills Billy. Ed Miller sees it and tells me, and I arrest him. That was my job, wasn't it? But she treats me like I was the criminal and him blameless. I wouldn't mind so much, but I love her. I've loved her for a long time."

And he had. He was rather old for her, but he loved her anyway. There weren't very many white women in Cinco County, and a thing like that could make a man awful woman-hungry.

"If she'd just say hello to me . . . ," he went on. "If she'd just show she knew I was *alive*. . . ." He lifted his head and glanced at me. Sweat was running down his face, but a drop or two of it could have been tears. "Couldn't you talk to her, Joe? Couldn't you tell her how it really was?"

I didn't have the heart to tell him I'd just talked to her about it. I didn't have the heart to tell him it was hopeless, so far as he was concerned.

"Give her a little time," I said. "It's still too fresh in her mind. Give her time, and then I'll see what I can do."

"I know you mean well, but couldn't you drop this thing? It'll never die down with you keeping it stirred up."

"We've been all through that. I already told you that, if you don't like it, you can ride back to Fort Benson."

"But why?"

I turned on him. "Because I want to sleep nights, that's why!" I shouted. "If I hanged an innocent man, I want to know. It's this damn' idea of not knowing for sure that. . . ." I caught hold of myself then. "I don't want to hear any more about it, Cal."

We saw the dust cloud, and then the riders came over the rise and headed down the slope toward us. Me and Cal reined in and waited for them. It was Spanish Bit.

Frank Tollison rode in the lead with four of his riders, fanning out behind him. I saw that one of the four was Johnny Rayburn. I knew them all. Me and Cal had worked with these boys.

Tollison reined in his white mare and patted his mustache and goatee. He fixed his eyes on me. "What's all this foolishness, Joe?" he asked.

"What do you mean, Mister Tollison?"

I looked at Johnny Rayburn, but he was staring down at his horse's ears.

"I hear you're stirring up this Roy Grant thing. You out of your head?"

"Who's been carrying you tales, Mister Tollison?"

"Never mind who. Is it true?"

I nodded.

"What's the idea?"

I got a grip on myself. I wasn't going to lose my temper. "I've been thinking," I said. "Everything was a little too pat against Grant. There's a lot of bad blood throughout the whole county because of that."

"And that bad blood will get worse with you poking around. I want you to stop it."

"I used to take orders from you, Mister Tollison, but I don't work for Spanish Bit any more."

He stiffened in the saddle. His right hand closed into a fist, and he brought it down on the saddle horn, but gently.

"I see. Very well, Joe. Would you mind telling me why you're keeping this thing stirred up?"

"There's a chance that Grant was innocent. He always said he was."

"They all say they're innocent. You ever know one who didn't? Dammit, man, Miller saw Grant kill Vesper. We all saw the butchered Spanish Bit steer. What more do you want?"

"I don't think Grant was the kind to butcher another man's beef."

"Half of Río Seco lives on butchered Spanish Bit beef. You know that. You know how all the two-bit ranchers hate our guts because we're the biggest outfit in Cinco County. Grant was no exception."

"It was all done pretty fast," I told him. "The trial one day and the hanging the next."

Tollison leaned forward in the saddle. "And what's wrong with that? It's always been done that way in Cinco County. If you're going to hang a man, why not get it over with?"

"What's your stake in this, Mister Tollison?"

"My stake?"

"That's right."

"Billy Vesper was one of my riders. I back my men one hundred percent. You know that, too."

"Did Billy ever have trouble with any of the other boys?"

He squinted at me. "Are you trying to say one of my own men killed Vesper?"

"That's not too unlikely. Billy was quarrelsome at times."

"What the hell was the butchered steer doing there, then?"

"A part of the frame."

Tollison poked a finger at me. "Listen, Joe. You're sheriff because Spanish Bit backed you. As long as you appreciate that fact, Spanish Bit will continue to back you. But if you want to go ahead on your own. . . ." He paused and drew a breath. "Let me tell you this. You're going to poke around until something comes to a head. It won't take much to start it. My riders go to Río Seco . . . the kids throw rocks at them . . . the women turn their backs on them, and the men won't talk unless they're spoken to. I've been holding my men back, but there's a limit to what I'll let them take. If harm comes to just one more of my men, I'm cleaning Río Seco out. Think on that for a while with what you use for a brain."

He spun the mare and touched it with his spurs. His boys took off after him. I watched them disappear over the rise, and then there was only their dust, and soon that was gone, too.

Cal said: "Where to now, Joe?"

"Miller's."

He sighed. "I was afraid of that."

I threw him a look, but he was staring off into the distance. After a while I started my roan. I didn't look to see if Cal was following, but soon I heard him come up at a trot behind me. We rode like that, without a word, all the way to Miller's.

We got to Miller's along about sundown. There were a couple of horses in a corral, but that was all. Ed Miller owned no stock. He no longer owned his ranch, either. The bank had foreclosed on it, but they let Ed stay on because they could find no one to buy the place.

The door was open, so me and Cal went right inside. There was just the one room. In a corner was a bunk, and Ed Miller was sleeping on it. He had gone to bed with a bottle, and, when he had dropped off, the bottle had tipped and spilled most of the liquor on the floor. I took the bottle and threw it outside. Then I shook Ed.

"Wake up," I said.

He had gone to sleep with all his clothes on. He hadn't even taken off his boots. I shook him, and he mumbled something, but his eyes stayed closed.

I shook him harder. "Come on, wake up."

His eyes batted this time and opened, and he lay there, blinking up at me.

"Time to rise and shine, Ed," I said.

He had a little trouble making me out at first. Finally he got me tallied. "Oh, it's you."

He sat up on the edge of the bunk and dropped his forehead in his hands. I gave him a couple of minutes, and then

I said: "Who buys your liquor for you, Ed?"

He blinked at me.

"I asked you who buys your liquor?"

He swallowed and licked his lips. "I do."

"With what?"

His eyes blinked. His mouth opened, but he said nothing.

"I want to know what you use for money," I said.

"I got money," Ed said.

"Yeah?"

"Sure I got money. All you people think I'm broke. Well, I got money, but I ain't telling no one how much."

"I'm not asking how much. I want to know where you get it."

He lifted a hand and rubbed his red-and-purple-splotched nose while he stared at me. He was not blinking so much any more. "I've just got it, that's all."

"Who gives it to you?"

"Who?" he repeated.

"That's right. Who?"

He waved a hand. "Why, I work a day here, a day there. That's who pays me."

"You're a liar."

He straightened a little. He started to get mad. "You got no call to say that. Just because you're sheriff, you got no right to come in my house. . . ."

"This is no longer your house. It's the bank's house. Tell me, Ed."

The starch went out of him. His shoulders sagged. "Tell you what?"

"Who gives you money?"

He stared down at the floor. He said nothing.

"Is it Spanish Bit?"

"Why would Spanish Bit give *me* money?"

"For having lied about Roy Grant."

I thought he started. His eyes went to Cal, begging for understanding there, then out the open door, then back to me. "I never lied about nothing," Ed said.

"I'm saying you have. Who on Spanish Bit is giving you money? Tollison?"

"Tollison?" Ed said. "Tollison wouldn't give me nothing. He's never had any use for me."

"Then it's someone else on Spanish Bit. Who?"

He hung his head sullenly. "No one gives me money. It's my own. I've had it from 'way back."

"You've got nothing from 'way back. You going to tell me the truth about Roy Grant?"

"I already told the truth. I told it in court."

"Yes, you told it, and Roy is dead. Is that why you're hitting the bottle so hard of late?"

"I like to drink. I always did. You know that."

"You never drank this much," I told him. "You never had enough money to drink this much, not even when you ran cattle. Where's the money coming from?"

"You think I done something wrong, arrest me and take me to Fort Benson. I want to see Judge Fitzpatrick or Ben Arnette, the prosecutor. Let them ask me questions."

I looked about the one room of his shack. On a shelf on the wall was a full whiskey bottle. I took it and walked to the door. I took careful aim at a rock in the yard and threw the bottle. As it smashed, Ed cried out.

I turned and went back to him. He had come to his feet. He stood trembling all over, his mouth working but only small, garbled sounds coming out.

"I'll get the truth from you, Ed," I told him. "I'm staying with you until I do. In the morning I'm taking you up into the Capitáns where Spanish Bit can't find us, and we're staying up there with nothing but water for you until you tell me what I want to know."

He didn't say anything. He threw himself on his bunk and covered his head with his arm.

I was so mad I had to step outside for a while. Cal came after me. I saw he had something on his mind. "Well?" I said. "What's eating you now?"

He spread his hands. "You know this is no good. Anything you get from Ed like this he can deny. It just won't hold up."

"I don't care if it doesn't hold up. At least, I'll know the truth. Once I know that, I'll get proof one way or another."

"You're spoiling everything, Joe. You've got Tollison against you now. A man ain't worth nothing in Cinco County with Tollison against him."

"That's my worry."

"I guess it is," Cal said. "Well, I tried. . . ."

Me and Cal decided to split the night in watching Ed Miller. I took the first half, and after midnight I woke Cal and told him to take over until dawn. Ed hadn't slept at all while I'd been awake. I guess it was the lack of whiskey that kept him from dropping off.

I was dog-tired, and I fell asleep right away. The shot woke me, and I sat up in my blankets, grabbing for my gun automatically while I blinked the sleep from my eyes. I could see that it was just turning gray outside.

The door was open and neither Cal nor Ed was in the shack. I hurried outside. Cal saw me come out the door, and he called to me. I went over to where he stood by the corral with Ed Miller limp and still on the ground.

Cal holstered his six-shooter as I came up. His face looked pale and strained. "I had no choice, Joe," he told me.

"Ed said he had to go outside, and I went with him. I don't know where he got the gun, but he must have had it hid in his bunk. Anyway, he turned on me, but I saw it coming."

I looked at Ed Miller, dead on the ground with a pistol just out of reach of his right hand. Then I looked up at Cal. I said: "A man kills once . . . he has to keep on killing, doesn't he, Cal?"

He looked at me sharp and hard. Then his eyes wavered a little, and he said: "What are you talking about?"

"You promised Ed you'd help him get away. You gave him a gun and brought him out here and then shot him. Isn't that how it was?"

He made a hurt face. "Why should I do a thing like that?"

"To keep Ed from telling me it was you giving him money."

His mouth grew tight and pinched at the corners. "Are you trying to say I killed Billy Vesper?"

"No. Ed probably killed Billy. Ed had been butchering Spanish Bit stock for quite some time. That's what you were doing up here when Billy got killed. I sent you to look into the stock killing. No, you didn't kill Billy, but you did kill Roy Grant."

"You're talking crazy, Joe."

"I don't think so. It was Ed that Billy caught, and, when you saw Ed kill Billy, you also saw a chance to get rid of Roy. So you made a deal with Ed. You'd shut up about him, and he'd say it was Roy who killed Billy. Roy had never got along too good with Spanish Bit. Then, too, Fitzpatrick and Arnette are Tollison's boys, so they were glad enough to railroad Roy to the gallows."

Cal's voice was barely a whisper. "Why would I want to frame Roy?"

"I don't think it's necessary to mention her name."

He didn't say anything for a little while. His eyes went past me to the Capitáns that were beginning to show in the distance and even beyond them to something that only he could see. His face turned old and tired. "You've got no proof," he said finally. "I'll just deny everything you say."

"I'll break you," I told him. "I've known you since we were kids, Cal, and I'll break you. I won't give you a minute's peace. I'll just keep hammering away. You've already taken it too hard. I'll hammer away until you break."

And that's how it was. He knew it was true, just as I knew it was true. I could have asked him for his gun because I'd always been a shade faster on the draw, but, when a man has to die, does it make any difference whether he's shot or hangs? And in Cal's case it would have been me as sheriff in either event. So I never said anything. I just waited there until he went for his gun.

Then he lay on the ground with his life's blood pumping out of his chest. He looked up at me with his eyes, begging me to understand. "I loved her, Joe," he said. "You'll never know how much I loved her. I sent an innocent man to his death, I loved her that much. I thought that with him gone, I'd have a chance with her. I never thought it would turn out like this. I'm sorry now. Will you tell her I'm sorry?"

"Tell that to Roy Grant, if you see him," I said, but Cal never heard me because he was already gone.

Endless Trail

He could see them waiting for him. In the twilight the cigarette made a soft, iridescent glow. Dan Burkett's steps slowed, halted, and that faint, indefinable fear touched him. He remained motionless in the path, watching the glow of the cigarette, seeing the black blotches of shadow the two men made against his cabin. For a moment Burkett knew the urge to turn back, but that would be running away again as he'd run on so many instances these past few weeks, and he'd never been the kind to run from anything.

It was one of those soft Alaskan evenings. The stars were just out, bright and very close overhead. A soft wind came sloughing through the pines and spruces, stirring the needles to a persistent whispering. To the north, moving across the sky in long, shimmering swaths, the aurora borealis began to play. This was so different, thought Burkett, from the endless, monotonous sweep of the wind over the flat Kansas prairie, the bitter, biting force of the wind driving across the Arizona high country in winter, or the fetid warmth of a breeze off the Nevada desert.

Burkett sighed and moved on up the path. They noticed him coming, and the murmur of their voices stilled.

In the silence, Burkett called out softly: " 'Evening, boys."

They returned his greeting. There were two of them. One was John Farrar, mayor of this settlement of Kiskiyu. A solid, chunky man in his late fifties, he sat with his back propped against the wall of the cabin Burkett was building.

Farrar had eyes of washed-out blue, and the look of a soulful dog about his wide mouth. But there was a contrasting firmness in the jut of his narrow chin.

His companion, Harry Axtell, who ran the general store, stamped out his cigarette. A tall, gaunt man, Axtell stood with drooping shoulders, hands shoved deeply in his pockets.

Burkett waited. He knew what was coming.

"I could begin by talking about the weather," Farrar said. "I could tell you what a fine cabin you're putting up, Dan. I could tell you that Hap Wilsey has made a strike up on the Little Musk-Ox. But you'd know that isn't what we're here for. So we'll get down to business."

Burkett nodded.

"I can't understand it, Dan," continued Farrar. "You've done it so many times in the past. It's been your life for I don't know how many years. I just can't understand it."

That was it, thought Burkett. No one could understand. Only he knew it down in the recesses of his heart, knew it in a cold, clammy, fearful way. To him, it was understandable, but it was a mute knowledge. He just couldn't find the words that would let others see it the way he saw it. He said it the way he'd said it several times before: "I'm through with that kind of life, John. I've put aside my gun for good. I just don't want to get back into it again."

Harry Axtell had shifted his hands into the hip pockets of his coat. "We're not asking that you become our permanent peace officer," he said. "We already have Bud Hubbard. It would only be for a few days, Dan. Hubbard can handle routine matters. It's just that he can't cope with Boomer Ferguson and his crowd. Ferguson is the key to it all. Run him out of Kiskiyu, and the hangers-on will follow. Ferguson won't run from Bud Hubbard, but he'll run from you."

Burkett swallowed a sigh. There was no use saying anything further. They couldn't look at it the way he did. They couldn't look inside him and see the gnawing fear that plagued him. Not fear of the danger — that was something alien to Burkett. Such a fear they might comprehend but not this other strange, compelling fright.

Farrar took it up again. "Look, Dan. You're settling down here. Before long, you'll be married. What kind of town do you want to live in? This town has no room for Ferguson and his kind. They're the scum that plague every frontier settlement. They've got to go before anything good and clean and decent can come from here. The families have moved in. They want a town that's free of gamblers and killers and painted women. Don't you want a town like that, Dan?"

Burkett's heart was heavy with sympathy for them, but there was no other way for him. "I'm sorry, John," he said finally. "I'm sorry."

After they had gone, Burkett turned from his half-finished cabin back up the slope to town. He intended calling on Lucy Carstairs this night as he called every night. He had considered himself fortunate in meeting her this late in life — in his early forties. His shoulders were broad and straight, and the litheness was still in his every move, but wisps of gray were beginning to tinge his temples.

Lucy was ten years his junior. She took in laundry and did sewing and mending for the miners and trappers. She was a good woman who would give him no regrets.

It would be a tremendous change for him, this settling down in one place to stay the rest of his life. He had run away from his farm home in Illinois, when he was sixteen, and had lived the vagabond life. The lure of new, fresh places had called to him, and he had never stayed in any one place too long. He'd helped drive a pack train to Santa Fé and had hunted buffalo. He'd prospected for silver in the Colorado highlands and driven a stagecoach, and then one day in Ellsworth he had faced down a gunman named Ben Thompson. That had been the beginning.

An endless parade of marshal's badges had graced his shirts. Ellsworth and Caldwell and Dodge, the roaring days in old Tombstone in Arizona and the silver and gold camps of Nevada. He'd brought law and order to countless towns, and, when it was all done, he'd packed his things and moved on.

Moved on until he had witnessed the death of the frontier West. Barbed wire dissected the great open ranges, and the roaring boom towns were a thing of the past. Then gold was discovered up in Alaska, opening a vast new wilderness to the avid, eager eyes of restless men, and, because that was the only thing he knew, Dan Burkett trailed north. There he met Lucy Carstairs.

The lights of the town were on Burkett. They came spilling softly out of the windows, laying their pattern on the dirt street. Ahead he could see the garish sign of Boomer Ferguson's Polar Bar. Burkett's blood began to quicken.

The quiet of the night was broken by the sounds from the Polar Bar, shattering the stillness and falling on Burkett's ears like balm. Someone was thumping a piano that sounded tinny and out of tune. There were singing voices and laughing voices and cursing voices. It was the frontier again, as he'd known it back in Dodge and Tombstone.

Burkett paused in front of the Polar Bar. He stood there with his eyes half closed, savoring the sound of it. This was the fear in him — the fear of the awful emptiness in him when the rootless, homeless horde should move on. This was his last link with the old days. He could come down here of an evening and lose himself again in the past. It made the dull, slow days bearable.

Burkett had started for the door when it opened suddenly, lamplight splashing Burkett, silhouetting him tall and tense against the darkness. He paused there as the two men emerged, stumbling and struggling.

The big man's struggles were dull with the stupor of too much drinking. He was making pawing, fumbling motions with his hands, striving to shield his head from the blows. The little man possessed the quick, startling movements of an attacking puma. He was all over the bigger fellow, his gun barrel striking sickening blows on the man's skull. Unbridled fury contorted the shorter man's face, made small, animal sounds in his throat.

Burkett halted. The big fellow was all done for. He no longer had the strength to lift his hands above his head. They hung weakly at his sides, fingers twitching convulsively at every blow. Blood matted his face, almost obliterating his features, but Burkett saw through the crimson, and with his recognition hot anger burst in his brain.

Leaping forward, Burkett closed steel fingers about the smaller man's shoulders, tore him away as the big fellow fell on his face.

"That's enough, Sanders, that's enough," growled Burkett.

Sanders whirled, gun poised. Burkett closed in swiftly, blocking the blow with his left shoulder, his right elbow coming up hard and cracking against Sanders's chin. The fellow's curse changed to a howl of pain. He went stumbling to the ground.

Sanders reached quickly for his fallen weapon. But

Burkett had jumped forward, towering above the other. Burkett's boot lifted, poised for a kick into the sitting man's stomach.

"Go on, Sanders," said Burkett. "Go ahead and try it."

Sanders's face turned sick in the lamplight that covered him. The heat died in his eyes, and his thin, narrow mouth began to twitch. Carefully he took his hand away. "You ain't heeled, Burkett," said Sanders, not quite able to keep the fright out of his tone. "I won't pull on a man that ain't heeled."

Burkett threw a scornful, derisive laugh at him. Sanders flushed, and his mouth moved to say more, but only a strangled sound came. He pushed himself to his feet, turned his back on Burkett, and began elbowing his way through the crowd that had gathered.

There were several men ringed around the fallen man.

"He sure got it good," said one of them.

"The man's hurt bad," said another. "He needs a doctor quick."

Four of them lifted the unconscious man and carried him off. Burkett watched until the night swallowed them. Then he turned into the Polar Bar.

He ordered a beer and stood with his elbows digging into the bar, hearing the sounds all around him — the jovial hum of voices, the vagrant snatches of song, the soft, delicate clicking of the chips from the faro layout and poker tables in the back of the place. But there was that other thing uppermost in Burkett's mind — the raw picture of Pete Ryan's battered, bloodied body lying on the ground.

It wasn't that this was anything new to Burkett, but Pete Ryan was the kind of man that Burkett was trying to be. Ryan had a wife and five kids. He had roots. He was like Farrar and Harry Axtell, the kind that stayed behind when the restless, homeless men shoved on.

There was an abrupt softening of the saloon sounds about him. It broke upon Burkett's reverie, and he raised his head to see the cause of it. He moved slowly forward, brown eyes staring above the heads of the crowd. The sounds stilled even more, and now the clacking of the poker chips in the rear was a harsh, grating noise. A man came from the rear, striding with firm, deliberate steps toward the town marshal.

This man was tall. His hair held the color and sheen of coal-black oil and the thick, well-trimmed black mustache accentuated the paleness of his features. The well-shaped mouth and a deep cleft in his chin, along with his large black eyes and long sideburns, made him a very handsome man. His black cutaway coat fitted his slim shoulders with tailored perfection and across his gaudy flowered vest glittered a gold watch chain. This was Boomer Ferguson.

Hubbard halted at the sight of Ferguson who cut over toward the bar, waiting insolently for Hubbard to come to him.

The marshal did not like this. His face flushed still more, but he approached Ferguson. "Where's Sanders?" he demanded.

Ferguson leaned an elbow indolently on the bar. "Am I supposed to be his keeper? How should I know?"

"Sanders works for you. Where are you hiding him?"

"Why don't you look around? It's what you're paid for, isn't it?"

Sweat drenched Hubbard's face. For a moment pity cut through the contempt in Burkett's heart. Hubbard was trying, but he just didn't have the guts.

"It's about Ryan," said Hubbard, half lamely, and Burkett felt a coldness squeeze his heart. "He's dead."

"So what?" said Ferguson. "He asked for it. He got drunk and started giving us all a bad time. He said the faro layout was fixed. He said the bartenders were shortchanging him and that one of the girls lifted his poke. When we cut the drinks off him and told him to go home, he got violent. Sanders had no choice."

Hubbard tried again. "Ryan was unarmed. Sanders had no call to gun whip him like that."

Ferguson's lip curled. "After all, Ryan was the bigger man. Sanders had to have something to equalize the odds. If Ryan had been reasonable, Sanders wouldn't have had to use force."

"All right," said Hubbard, drawing himself up, trying to bluster his way out of it. "I'll let it ride this time, but don't let it happen again. Another time I'm gonna crack down, by God."

Ferguson smiled mockingly. "Sure, Marshal. Whatever you say, Marshal."

The flavor was gone from his beer, and Burkett left it half finished on the bar and walked out. Outside he paused a moment, watching the play of the aurora borealis across the northern sky, troubled thoughts starting to torment him again.

He struck off down the street at a slow walk, head bowed in thought, and he almost ran into Farrar.

"Thank God I've found you, Dan," said Farrar.

He was breathing hard as if he'd been running. He reached out a hand, grasping Burkett's arm, fingers digging in urgently. "I'm trying once more, Dan. Harry and the others said it was no use, but I've got to try once more. They're through taking it. They're striking back."

Because it was there already in his mind, torturing him with its insistence, a ragged irritation flowed through

Burkett. He was beginning to understand how it stood with him, how it would always stand with him, and with all his heart he didn't want it that way.

"Make sense, John," he said shortly.

Farrar drew a deep breath. "Harry's called a meeting to organize a vigilance committee. He's a hothead. He'll get more hotheads to back him, and then they'll head for Ferguson and Sanders. But that isn't the way, Dan. Vigilantes have a way of getting out of hand. There's no telling where they'll stop and draw the line."

They came storming through Burkett's mind now, all the doubts, all the nagging fears. Everything in his mind cried out against it, but the fear kept him chained.

"All that it will take is one word from you, Dan. Deep down inside they're all yellow. I heard how Sanders quit cold on you tonight, even though he had a gun and you were unarmed. They'll heed you. You're the only one here that can save a lot of useless bloodshed."

Mingled with the fear in Burkett was a sudden anger at himself, at the weakness against which he was so powerless. There was a slight, barely perceptible tremble in his voice. As always, he knew what he had to do.

"All right, John," he said.

Farrar's breath tore out of him in a relieved gasp. "Thanks, Dan. You don't know what this means to us. I'll go tell Harry and the boys, and we'll swear you in as deputy."

Burkett's voice was heavy. "I want to go and tell Lucy first. Then I'll be along."

He had had all the right words framed in his mind, but when the telling of it came, it was a jumbled, incoherent mess. He tried to get it out, tried so hard that little beads of sweat broke out on his brow, but the words just wouldn't come.

Lucy Carstairs listened with her head inclined a little, seemingly intent on her sewing. She had a rather plain face that was smoothly round and marked by large, gentle brown eyes.

When Burkett got to the nagging fears roiling inside him, he could go no further. To him it had always been clear enough, but could she understand? Could anyone understand?

"So I thought I'd come and tell you, Lucy," he finished. "I wanted you to know and to have your consent."

She smiled gently. "Of course, you have my consent, Dan. It's something that has to be done. It should have been done long ago."

He wanted it out of him so badly he tried again. "You don't understand, Lucy. It's more than that. I'm trying to tell you how it is. I . . . I don't want to do it. I quit that sort of thing, and I don't want to go back to it."

Her head lifted, face sober and querying. "If it's because of me, you needn't worry. I know you meant it, when you promised you'd quit the old ways and settle down. I know this is different."

"They kept nagging me," continued Burkett huskily. "They wouldn't let me alone. It was nag, nag, nag until they broke me down."

"It's all right, Dan," she said simply.

"Then you really don't mind?" he asked, feeling the weight of it still pressing down on him.

"Mind?" she asked, a soft smile on her lips. "I'm proud, Dan. I'm proud that they turned to you as the one man who could help them."

Maybe it wouldn't be so bad, after all, he told himself after he left Lucy. Maybe after they'd been driven away and the last link had been broken, he could forget. He'd have his home and Lucy, and perhaps he could settle down.

He went to his boarding house and dug down into his pack for his .44 Starr Army revolver. He checked it over carefully, loading the cylinder, then buckling the old, worn shell belt and holster about his waist.

He made short work of being sworn in. Pinning a deputy's badge to his shirt, he left them immediately, spurning their offers to back him up with armed force.

The night seemed chill to Burkett. The stars looked cold and close overhead, and the aurora borealis was a brilliant, weaving display across the heavens. The heavy, filled holster knocked softly against his thigh as he walked along, and it brought all the old feelings back to him, doubly strong now after such a long denial. He felt a quickening in his blood and a surging buoyancy in his walk.

The sounds from the Polar Bar came drifting down the street to him. They were fuller now, with an urgent, savage, restless undertone to them. He came to the Polar Bar and was across the street when he noticed the man in the shadows. The glow of the man's cigarette gave him away, flaring and fading with a faint regularity like the slow, dull beatings of a dying heart.

Burkett halted, digging his heels into the dirt of the street. His voice held none of his tight, pent-up feelings.

"Hello, Ferguson."

Ferguson did not answer right away. Burkett could feel the speculative weight of his eyes. After a long pause, Ferguson let out his breath in a sigh and dropped his cigarette.

"It *is* true," he said at length. "They said you were taking a badge again, but I didn't believe it. I was sure you had put all that behind you, but now the badge is there on your shirt, and I guess you mean it all right. What made you change, Burkett?"

"Pete Ryan was my friend."

Ferguson's laugh held a soft, mocking edge. The shadows blanketed him. Burkett could see only the pale blot made by the man's face and vague outlines of his body.

"You've never been a sentimentalist, Burkett," said Ferguson. "It goes deeper than that. You just couldn't stay away from it. Isn't that it? Ryan is just a handy alibi. You couldn't stay away from it any more than I could settle down and stop running a joint."

A faint irritation began stirring in Burkett. He didn't like having it brought out like this. He said gruffly: "I didn't come to pass the time of day, Ferguson."

"No, I didn't think you did. But before we go off half cocked, couldn't we talk it over?"

"I've never made deals with your kind."

Ferguson sighed. "I know you haven't. Still, I thought that now that you're getting on in years, maybe you could see it differently. You're mature now, Burkett. Averting your eyes now and then is a prudent thing to do."

Burkett shook his head. "I'm too old to change my ways."

"Well? What did you want with me, then?"

"You ought to know. You've been run out of other towns."

"A man gets tired of running," said Ferguson, and something primal flared in his tone. "A man gets tired of being pushed around. It'll come to that sooner or later, so it might as well be now."

Ferguson had been doing something with his left hand, and suddenly a match glared into flame in his fingers. The impact of it hit Burkett hard, and, even as the truth unfolded for him, he was twisting, ducking, hand driving for the butt of his .44 Starr.

This would be Ferguson's way, and Burkett cursed his carelessness. The pattern of it had been evident enough. Ferguson, waiting in the shadows, biding his time in that gulfing darkness — the darkness that might conceal a back-shooting killer like Sanders.

Even as the thought was bursting in his mind, flame split the solid wall of blackness. He heard the whistle of the slug pass him. The .44 Starr was in his hand, and he had the burst of gunflame to guide his bullets. He laid down two rapid shots.

An animal-like scream hit his ears, blending harshly with the echoes of gunfire, but there was still the menace of Ferguson behind him. Burkett whirled, the hammer of his gun eared back.

Ferguson's hand was coming out from beneath his left armpit.

Burkett fired once.

He checked Sanders first and found him dead. Returning to the front of the Polar Bar carrying Ferguson, he pushed through the throng that had gathered and dropped on his knees beside the gambler.

The man was dying. A wax-like pallor lay over his features, and his breath came in laboring gasps. Burkett watched him, and, as he stared, a strange pity came over him.

"I'm sorry, Boomer," said Burkett. "I've destroyed your world, at the same time destroying mine. I've always done that. I've always helped destroy the only way of life I know."

"You're a queer one," said Ferguson with his last breath. "I could never make you out before. But now I think I understand. . . ."

* * * * *

Burkett had given them — the restless, ruthless, rootless ones — their ultimatum, and now, the next morning, he sat on a knoll, watching their exodus from Kiskiyu. As Burkett watched, he felt the frightening emptiness descend on him. He knew a moment of panic, and, as the sweat broke out on his brow, he realized the truth. He had thought that he could endure it, but now he knew sadly that it wasn't so. He felt the pull again, the pull of those invisible horizons.

That evening, as he walked through the town, he sensed that something was missing. He thought a while, and then he knew that what was lacking was the sound of the wild revelry from the Polar Bar.

His decision was made. Back at his boarding house, Burkett prepared a light pack which he slung over his shoulders. He went out into the night and walked to where Lucy Carstairs lived.

"I'm leaving, Lucy," he told her. "It's what I was afraid of last night. You see, I don't fit in here any more. I get scared whenever I stop and look into the future. It's a life I don't know how to live."

She smiled sadly. "It's your decision, Dan."

He wanted very much to make her see it the way he saw it, but still the words just stumbled around in his mind. "I tried to tell you," he repeated defensively. "Do you understand, Lucy?"

"I understand your kind," she said.

"I'd ask you to go along," he said, "but it's an endless trail I'm following. I'll never stay fixed any place long. I wouldn't make you happy, and knowing that, and knowing that it was my weakness making it like that, I'd come to blame you for it and maybe even hate you. I wouldn't want things to work out like that."

There was much more to say, all the regrets and sadness inside him, but the saying of it was beyond his capacity.

"Good bye, Lucy," he said.

"Good bye, Dan."

Then he was off, his pack on his back, stepping along with long, swift strides. He felt an urge to turn and look back, but a certain pride held him from doing so. He kept his eyes ahead. To the north the aurora borealis had begun to play.

Riders of the Shadowlands

I

On a job for the Cattle Growers Association, Gatewood rode south to the Doloritas country, just north of the border. The Doloritas is a range of contradictions. There are barren, sterile crags, low-hung peaks that jut sullenly up at the yellow sky, and yet there are certain spurs and ridges that are green with timber and graze. Gatewood was riding through one of these when he came upon the four men.

Three of them were so intent on what they were doing that they were unaware of Gatewood as he came up behind them. As for the fourth, he, too, had no knowledge of Gatewood, but this one was in no position to know anything except the pain from the quirt lashes on his bare and bleeding back.

There was one cedar in the middle of a small clearing, and the man was bound to this with his arms around the trunk and his wrists tied together. His body stiffened and writhed with each cruel blow of the quirt, but no cry came from his lips. He had his head dropped back and on one side, and his upper teeth were clenched down over his lower lip so that blood trickled. Although each blow brought a spasm of pain across his face, he made no sound.

The man wielding the quirt was tall and blond. A bestial pleasure glittered in his eyes, and it was clearly evident that he would rather be doing a thing like this than anything else in the world. His lips were drawn back from his teeth in a grimace of brutal glee, and he kept bringing his arm way back and then swinging it up and down with all the strength he possessed. His exertions had brought out a fine film of sweat on his face and had wetted his shirt under the arm-pits.

The other two watched with an avid preoccupation. They were both dressed as cowpunchers, and their horses as well as two others were off to one side. Only the horses were indifferent to what was going on, calmly munching the grass.

Gatewood came on quietly, his black mare making no sound on the grass. Sight of what was going on did not trouble Gatewood too much. He was twenty-eight years old, and he had been working for the Association for five years. In that time he had run across a considerable amount of cruelty and greed and downright rottenness in men, so that he was never surprised at what he encountered, no matter how bizarre or brutal it might be.

He stood an even six foot, although slouched over in the saddle, as he was now, he appeared to be somewhat shorter. He had red hair that crept, uncut, down over the tops of his ears and a red stubble of beard lining his rather gaunt cheeks and beginning to conceal the cleft in his chin. His eyes were a pale blue, and the cynicism he felt inside showed in their skeptical glitter and in the slightly bitter curve of his mouth.

He took out his .44 Frontier Colt and held it with the long seven-and-a-half-inch barrel resting against his thigh as he reined in the black mare behind the two cowpunchers who were so eagerly watching.

Gatewood said: "You're liable to throw your arm out of joint, bucko, working so hard like that. Why don't you lay off for a while until you're rested? Then you can start in again."

The man doing the whipping froze just as he had begun to bring his arm down with another lash, and he wheeled around with his arm held high like that, the crimson tip of the quirt dangling limply against his shoulder. The two cowpunchers spun, stabbing their hands at the butts of their six-shooters, but Gatewood snapped up his .44 and racked back the hammer, and the cold, angry purpose in his eyes deterred the two.

The man with the quirt was slowly lowering his right hand, bringing it down carefully but with a calculated purpose, since he was behind one of the cowpunchers. Gatewood jumped the mare ahead a step so that he could cover the man with the quirt adequately.

Gatewood said tightly: "Go ahead, bucko. I'm not stopping you. Go ahead and pull your iron."

The man's right hand froze waist-high while his eyes took a second, more considerate, appraisal of Gatewood. Then the man with the quirt lifted his right hand once more until his fingers were shoulder-high.

"Turn your backs to me," said Gatewood, "and drop your gun belts, one by one. You in the red shirt first, then you, bucko, with the chaps, and finally you with the quirt. Try something funny, and you might get away with it, and then again you might not. Well?"

The two cowpunchers looked inquiringly at the man with the quirt. They would obviously do anything he commanded, but he had thought it over and considered how this stranger's gun was meant first for him, and so he shrugged and turned around. The two cowpunchers followed suit, and in the order which Gatewood had stipulated they unbuckled their shell belts and dropped their holstered six-shooters to the ground.

Now that he was unarmed, the man with the quirt felt it

was safe to object. "You don't know what you're getting into, stranger," he said quietly, but with a threatening undertone. "You don't know anything about this, and you're making a big mistake, taking sides. If I were you, I'd put up my gun, and I'd ride right on away from here."

"Cut him loose," said Gatewood, motioning with his .44 to the man bound to the tree.

The man with the quirt stiffened. His eyes glittered. "I'm telling you again, stranger. This is none of your business. Keep your nose. . . ."

Sudden wrath suffused Gatewood's face. He reared up in his stirrups and leveled his .44 at the other's belly. The cords stood out in Gatewood's neck as he shouted: "Cut him loose, you stinking yellow-belly! I don't care what your business is or which side is the right side. When I see three men working over another who's helpless, that's enough for me. Cut him loose. Quick!"

The man with the quirt took in the lethal and competent thrust of the .44 in Gatewood's hand and, with a perceptible effort, swallowed his ire and walked over to the cedar. With quick, sullen motions he loosened the ropes.

The man at the tree almost went down on his knees when the rope no longer supported him. He clutched at the trunk to keep from going all the way down, and then with a great effort he pulled himself back up on his feet. Tentatively, he stepped back from the cedar.

Once again his knees almost buckled, but he found the strength to hold himself upright. Without glancing at anyone, he went over to where his shirt lay on the ground. He picked up his shirt and gingerly draped it across his shoulders, knotting the sleeves beneath his chin. Then he faced Gatewood.

This man stood about two inches under six feet. He had

broad, powerful shoulders, a barrel-like torso, and the narrow waist and flat hips of a horseman. His face was round and pleasant, and, although it was strained with pain, he managed a small smile.

"Thanks, friend," he murmured.

Then he turned his glance on the blond man who had whipped him. The man's eyes went chill, and the muscles bulged along his jaw.

"I don't feel up to it right now," he said, "but there'll come a day, Farrell."

The man with the quirt showed a mirthless, jibing smile. "Any time, Stallcup, any time," he said quietly, but with the same ugly undertone he had used with Gatewood.

Stallcup now walked over to the four grazing horses, and it was then that Gatewood noticed that three of the animals wore the Stirrup brand while the horse Stallcup mounted had a 33 mark burned in its hide. Stallcup rode his horse, a roan, over beside Gatewood's mare.

"Should we go, friend?" he asked.

"No," said Gatewood. "I think I'll ride on with these three boys. I've got business at Stirrup."

Stallcup looked puzzled. His shell belt and holstered Remington .44-40 was hanging from his saddle horn, and now he slowly belted on the weapon, studying Gatewood all the while out of narrowed, inquiring eyes. Finally Stallcup shrugged and reined his roan away.

"Suit yourself, friend," he said. He laid a long, ominous look on Farrell, and then kicked the roan with the spurs and went off at a hard run, quickly disappearing into the timber.

Gatewood stared at Farrell, wondering how to put it into words. Gatewood had had no idea that these were Stirrup riders, and now he realized ruefully he could not have got off to a worse start on this job. He holstered his .44 and said: "My name's Gatewood. I'm an inspector for the Cattle Growers Association. A man named Renshaw, from Stirrup, sent for me."

Farrell's jaw dropped. For a moment he looked ludicrous with the gaping, vacant cast of the idiot on his features. Then sudden fury mottled his face, and he barked out an obscene word.

"Well, this is rich," he snarled. "This is really rich. You're gonna be a great help, Gatewood."

Gatewood felt his face flush. "All right, all right," he growled. "So I got off on the wrong side of the horse. That's over and done with. Let's get on with what lies ahead of us."

"That's just what I was doing," shouted Farrell, "until you butted in and played the devil with everything."

The two cowpunchers had by now belted on their six-shooters again. One of them picked up Farrell's shell belt and handed it to the man. With an angry gesture Farrell grabbed the belt but made no move to buckle it on.

Gatewood folded his hands over the saddle horn. His lips were stiff with the anger he was trying to contain within himself. "Let's get the tally straight, Farrell," he said thinly. "This Renshaw I mentioned is a member of the Cattle Growers Association. His dues are all paid up. When he wrote in to the Association requesting an inspector because his Stirrup cows were being rustled, I was sent here. My business is with Renshaw. I don't have to take any dirt from hired hands."

Farrell's chest swelled. "Hired hands?" he bellowed. He began beating his breast with a fist. "*I'm* Stirrup. I ramrod Stirrup. I do the hiring and the firing. I run the whole she-bang. Me, Steve Farrell, *I'm Stirrup!*"

"Doesn't Renshaw have anything to do with it?" Gatewood asked dryly. "I thought he owned Stirrup."

"Mister Renshaw owns Stirrup, but I run it, Gatewood, and I can keep on running it without outside interference. Mister Renshaw wanted the Association brought into this. I didn't. I can handle those rustlers in my own way without troubling the Association. And I was doing that very thing until you stepped in. Do you know who Wade Stallcup is? He's one of the rustlers you were sent to find. But what did you do, instead? You set him loose just when I had started to teach him that it doesn't pay to rustle Stirrup beef.

"Is this how you operate, Gatewood? I expected something like you from the Association and that's why I didn't want anyone sent here, but Mister Renshaw felt that, as long as he's always paid his dues, he might as well get something in return for his money." Farrell's scathing look raked Gatewood. "Well, he certainly got it."

Gatewood didn't know how long he could keep himself in check, but he went on trying, although he would much rather have jumped the mare ahead into Farrell and sent the man sprawling on his sneering face.

"I must admit you have a unique way of handling rustlers," said Gatewood. "Whipping them to death *is* one way of getting rid of them, but it's hardly legal, is it? Another thing, did you catch Stallcup in the act of running off some Stirrup beef?"

"I caught him on Stirrup ground and that's enough for me," Farrell said defiantly. "He's been warned to stay off Stirrup. He knew what he was getting into when he rode on Stirrup ground. And let me tell you something, Gatewood. You aren't gonna catch Stallcup or anyone else in the act of running off Stirrup beef.

"I can tell you who the rustlers are. Wade Stallcup, Lonnie Grissom, Amos Clark, Red Daniels. I don't need an inspector from the Association to find that out. But what good does it do knowing who the rustlers are when you can't do anything about it because you haven't got any proof that will stand up in court? What am I supposed to do, sit on my rump while they keep on running off Stirrup beef?

"I'll tell you what I'm going to do. I'm giving every one of them the same treatment I gave Stallcup. I'm beating them to within an inch of their lives, and, if that isn't warning enough for them to lay off Stirrup beef, there's going to come the day that they'll all be swinging from a cedar somewhere in the Doloritas! That's the way to handle rustlers, not the namby-pamby Association way!"

Gatewood was suddenly weary of it. He realized nothing would come of arguing with Farrell. Besides, Gatewood had come a long way that day, and he was tired, and he wanted to get to Stirrup and see Renshaw and then rest a while before taking on this job in the morning.

"I'm not going to stay here gabbing with you all afternoon, Farrell," said Gatewood. "If you'll point out the shortest way to Stirrup, I'll be going."

II

Farrell and the two cowpunchers rode with Gatewood, and the four of them reached Stirrup headquarters at sundown. The ranch buildings lay on a small rise in the middle of the lushest, richest valley Gatewood had yet come across in the Doloritas. The valley walls that sloped up into the rugged crests were covered with timber. There was a small creek that began somewhere up in the mountains and which flowed placidly through the center of this valley.

Other riders were coming in from various points in the

valley, all of them converging on Stirrup's buildings. As they came into the ranch yard, Farrell suggested to Gatewood that he eat before meeting Renshaw. Farrell pointed out that Renshaw ate in the house with his daughter and his housekeeper while the hands ate in the bunkshack. Farrell had calmed considerably during the long ride down from the mountain, although he still carried a hostile and aloof air about him. He had not spoken once during the ride until now.

That was all right with Gatewood. He had taken an instant dislike to Farrell and realized that it would not be a pleasant task, working with the man, and, for that reason, Gatewood hoped that his stay here at Stirrup would not be for long. Farrell made no explanation about Gatewood to the Stirrup riders. While they ate, Farrell pointedly ignored Gatewood. When they were done, Farrell stated he would takc him up to the house.

The man's arrogant, overbearing manner did not sit well with Gatewood, but he decided, in the interest of amity, to overlook it. So he followed Farrell into the big house, into a room that was obviously used as the office at Stirrup.

There was a roll-top desk in one corner, and the walls were adorned with mounted trophies. There were the snarling heads of three mountain lions and the head of an elk and an immense brace of longhorns. There was also a Stirrup branding iron that was affixed to the center of one wall like a seal of authority. Arranged around the branding iron was a ring of old cap-and-ball revolvers and a pair of handsome dueling pistols.

Gatewood noticed the redolent smell of good tobacco smoke. The man who was smoking sat in a chair by the desk, his left leg thrust out stiff and straight, a cane within reach of his hand. He was a tall, gaunt man with a resigned and patient sadness in the lines of his face. This was Buck Renshaw, owner of Stirrup.

Standing off to one side was the girl. Gatewood noticed that she was rather tall and slim and that her blonde hair was gathered in a bun on the back of her neck. There was a strong family resemblance between her and Renshaw: the same thin nose, the same wide, pleasant mouth, the same cool, gray eyes. She made a striking picture, her beauty all the more enhanced by the white blouse and plain blue skirt she was wearing.

Farrell walked over beside the girl, his aloofness gone, smiling, even fawning, as he called her Miss Ellerine. Gatewood found himself resenting this, although he could not understand why, unless it was because of his thorough dislike of Farrell.

"This is Gatewood, Mister Renshaw," said Farrell. "He's from the Association."

Renshaw reached out, and Gatewood shook hands with him. He could feel those gray eyes weighing him, considering him, gauging his competence, a cautious reserve in them that held a hint of skepticism.

"Pleased to have you, Gatewood," said Renshaw.

He had his pipe in his hand, and now he set it down on his desk. The look in his eyes said that he would not accept Gatewood until he had proven himself.

"There's no need for me to go into details with you," Renshaw said quietly. "Steve will do that. He has a better first-hand knowledge of them than I have." A touch of regret and heart-aching longing came into his voice. "You see, I . . . don't get around so much any more."

Gatewood could not keep his glance from touching briefly the man's left leg. Renshaw had the look of a man who had been born in the saddle, but those days were gone for him. The trophies on the walls attested to another great passion in his life that must now be limited, if not abrogated entirely. That could be the cause of the sadness on Renshaw's face, but, somehow, Gatewood felt that it was due to something more than this.

"I want those rustlers not only caught but convicted and sent to prison," Renshaw went on. "Do you think you can do that, Gatewood?"

"That's what the Association pays me for."

Farrell snorted derisively. Gatewood felt his face get warm. With an effort he kept his eyes on Renshaw, although the words were directed at Farrell.

"Catching the rustlers shouldn't be too difficult. Getting the evidence for a conviction is something else again."

"This isn't going to do any good, Mister Renshaw," Farrell broke in. "We don't need the Association. This man isn't going to help any. Leave it to me. We won't be bothered by these rustlers much longer. I'm making progress."

"Like this afternoon, for instance?" asked Gatewood.

"Yes. Like this afternoon," he said stiffly, defiantly.

Renshaw cleared his throat. His voice was mollifying. "You've had a hard day, Steve. I won't keep you here any longer, if there's something you have to do before you turn in. Why don't you take Ellerine with you? I want to chat with Gatewood a while and make him feel at home. It's nothing about Stirrup. You can go into that with Gatewood in the morning, Steve."

Farrell glared at Gatewood a moment longer and then said brusquely: "Coming, Ellerine?"

There was something possessive about his tone that once more fanned resentment in Gatewood. He glanced at the girl and saw that she had colored a little, but she followed Farrell to the door. As she passed Gatewood, she laid a long, cool, speculative stare on him, and he returned it. She did not seem to mind it, and her mouth just started to curve in the hint of a smile when she was past him and then gone out of the door after Farrell.

Renshaw was sucking on his pipe again and staring at the floor. "You don't seem to hit it off with Steve," he observed quietly.

Gatewood shrugged. "Every man has his likes and dislikes," he said.

Renshaw drew deeply on his pipe, then smiled deprecatingly. "Sure, Steve resents your coming here, but that's just natural. He takes it as a slight on his ability. I've explained to him that I belong to the Association, and I pay my dues, and I want something in return for the money I've paid out. But he's taken it into his head that you're here because he can't handle the rustlers. You should take his side of it into consideration.

"Steve is a good man, one of the best ramrods in the country. His devotion to Stirrup is something you don't find very often in a foreman, Gatewood. Stirrup is Steve's whole life. I need a man like him . . . now that I don't get around much any more."

The sadness came back on his face and the wistfulness in his voice, and, again, Gatewood had the feeling that these were just superficial things. The root of the matter seemed to go much deeper than a crippled leg and the termination of a way of life.

"I'll do the best I can," said Gatewood. "I'll go out of my way to get along with Farrell because that's my job, but I don't take dirt from anyone."

Renshaw was staring at the floor once more, seemingly immersed deeply in some melancholy, secret recollection. He did not appear to have heard. Then he roused himself enough to dismiss Gatewood with a small wave of his hand. He was still staring at the floor as Gatewood left the room.

Gatewood came outside and saw where Ellerine Renshaw and Farrell were standing by a corner of the house. It was now night, and in the shadows Farrell's cigarette glowed red. Gatewood paused a moment, staring at the two, not understanding what it was that held him here, for certainly whatever it was between these two was none of his business.

Finally Farrell said dryly: "Looking at something, Gatewood?"

Gatewood moved over in front of Farrell and the girl. Again he was conscious of the girl's interest in him. It was something unspoken, yet real and tangible.

"Does a man have to get your permission before he can stare in any given direction, Farrell?"

Anger pulled Farrell's lips thin. The cigarette glowed very red, then faded as he took it from his mouth. He pointed the smoke at Gatewood, jabbing it forward now and then by way of emphasis.

"Let me tell you something. You might work for the Cattle Growers Association, but you're also employed by Stirrup. I ramrod Stirrup, and as long as you're working here, even if you draw your pay from the Association, you take orders from me. In the morning I'll explain the whole situation to you, and I'll take you around and show you what I've found out. But in all this you're working for Stirrup, understand? You're just one of the hired hands."

"Like you, Farrell?" asked Gatewood softly.

The man cast the cigarette violently from him. If it hadn't been for the presence of the girl, Gatewood was sure he would have had a fight on his hands. Farrell said something sharply to the girl, wheeled, and stalked off into the house. She followed, again giving Gatewood that long, considerate look, and she must have been pleased about something, for as she went past she smiled at him over her shoulder.

III

Now the work began for Gatewood. It was Farrell's belief that the rustlers picked up a few cows at a time, driving them to some isolated, hidden spot in the Doloritas where the animals were held until a number of them had been acquired, then these would be run across the border on some suitable night and sold in Mexico. Gatewood was inclined to go along with this idea, for there had been no report of any attempt to run off a large herd at one crack, and there also didn't seem to be any indication of brand altering.

So Gatewood took to prowling the Doloritas in an effort to pick up some sign of where the stolen cattle were being driven. He took along enough supplies so that he would not have to run in to Stirrup for at least a week.

In three days Gatewood had no luck at all. He covered the slopes of the Doloritas; he explored the timber; he looked into cañons and barren, isolated valleys. He studied and peered until his eyes ached. The whiskers lengthened on his face, and he became saddle-sore and tired and mean, as nothing turned up.

Then, in the middle of the fourth day as he was emerging from a box cañon after another fruitless search, he saw the three riders coming in on him. The land here was flat, dotted with sage and mesquite, and the riders raised a small spume of dust as they came on at a trot. Gatewood comprehended that this was for him, and so he reined in the black mare and waited for the others to come up. Pushing his hat back on his head, he mopped his sweating face, all the while studying the riders as they came closer. There was something deliberate and coldly calculated in the way they fanned out as they approached, so as to come in on him from three sides.

A chill caught the back of Gatewood's neck, and he put his bandanna in a hip pocket and yanked his hat down to take the sun out of his eyes, and his right hand loosened the .44 in its holster. He sat there motionless in the saddle, as the three horsemen came up, ringing him in with a cool, lethal precision.

The three halted their horses and stared at Gatewood a while, none of them saying anything. The middle one was a short, paunchy redhead, his hat shoved back a little to show his receding hairline. He had big, freckled hands which he folded over his saddle horn.

The one on Gatewood's right was a youth, no more than twenty, tall and gangly, with gelid gray eyes. He seemed openly contemptuous as he looked Gatewood up and down. There was a hardness about this one's mouth and a grim competence in the hang of the six-shooter at his side that belied his youthfulness. The third rider was an old fellow dressed in soiled, smelly buckskins. Dirty gray whiskers covered his face, and his hair hung long and uncut down the back of his neck. He was grinning as he gazed at Gatewood, but there was an emptiness and a lack of purpose to it.

Finally the redhead spoke. "You're doing a sight of riding here in the Doloritas. Why?"

Gatewood glanced about him, at the youth's cool contempt, at the old-timer's vapid grin, then back to the redhead's insistent eyes. "Maybe I like the exercise," he said quietly.

Irritation crossed the redhead's face. "Don't try to get funny, Gatewood. We know who you are and what you're here for. Stirrup sent for you, and you can get straight back to Stirrup. Any riding you've got to do you can do on Stirrup ground. Is that clear?"

"Whose ground is this I'm on right now?" asked Gatewood. "Yours?"

"All you need to know is that it doesn't belong to Stirrup. The Doloritas is no place for an Association inspector. Go back where you came from, if you know what's good for you!"

"Look, bucko, I'm a working man just like anybody else. I don't step on anybody's toes just because I happen to work for the Association. I've got a job to do here, and I intend to stick around until it's finished. I got nothing against you, bucko. Why should you have anything against me?"

"Hasn't Farrell told you about us, Gatewood?" the redhead asked. "I'm Red Daniels. That's Lonnie Grissom, and the old-timer is Amos Clark. Hasn't Farrell told you it's us who are running off Stirrup beef? We're the little fellows. We're the ones to be pushed around by the big outfits like Stirrup. We're the ones to be given every dirty, rotten name in the business. Well, we're not going to stand for anything like that. We're not going to be framed for something we didn't do. Is that clear?"

"You've got it all wrong, Daniels," Gatewood said placatingly. "I'm not trying to frame anybody. As for Farrell, he's not telling me how to do my job. I don't care what Farrell's suspicions are. All I'm interested in is proof. If you three boys are in the clear, you have nothing to be afraid of from me."

"Rotten, stinking sneak!"

It was the youth, Grissom. Gatewood felt his throat constrict. He looked at Grissom and read the hot, defiant challenge in the boy's eyes. Gatewood glanced the other way at the old-timer and experienced a chill when he saw that the fellow's grin was no longer automatic and empty but full of a foul eagerness.

"What's the matter, Gatewood?" Daniels asked, voice jibing, mocking. "The kid is right, isn't he? You sneak around. That's your job, isn't it? You've been sneaking around the Doloritas for several days now."

"Sneak," Grissom hissed. "Low-down, yellow-bellied sneak."

Gatewood realized that there wasn't much he could do now. They had him ringed in. They would prod him, needle him until he lost his head and went for his gun. They were three to one, and they didn't mind at all if he pulled his iron first. Until that moment came, they intended having some fun, pushing him around.

Grissom jumped his horse ahead, smashing the animal against the mare's rump, and she squealed and almost went down on her knees. Gatewood reined her up and around so that he faced Grissom, conscious that Daniels had moved around behind him. They were making sure one of them was always behind him.

"Sneak, sneak!" Grissom cried. "Crawling, gutless sneak!"

Although he knew he was playing into their hands, Gatewood felt an overwhelming urge to strike at the three. They had him outnumbered. He couldn't hope to get all of them, but, if he got one, or maybe two, that would be enough to satisfy him.

He was just setting himself to reach for his .44 when the voice cried out: "Break it up!"

Grissom had been waiting impatiently for Gatewood to

start his pass at his weapon, and, at the sound of the cry, Grissom's head flung up, and he wheeled his horse around to catch sight of the one who had spoken. It was Stallcup.

Stallcup was sitting hunched forward in his saddle, his mouth pulled down at the corners in anger. The black butt of his six-shooter showed in the holster at his side. Defiance blazed in Grissom's face, and he reined his horse back around, jumping it ahead again in another effort to smash into Gatewood's mare.

"I said break it up!" shouted Stallcup.

He sent his roan ahead with a sudden lunge, reaching out and grasping the bridle of Grissom's horse, pulling up the animal before it could touch the mare. Then, swiftly, Stallcup released the bridle and brought the flat of his hand across Grissom's face.

"What do you want me to do?" Stallcup cried. "Translate it into border Spanish and all the Apache dialects before you understand? I said break it up!"

Grissom was holding the side of his face. His eyes grew sullen, but he slowly turned his horse away. Then, in a sudden fit of anger, he raked the animal sharply with the spurs, sending it at a hurtling run across the land.

Daniels had his gun in his hand. He kept glancing from Gatewood to Stallcup. He could not reconcile what was going on, and his perturbation showed plainly on his face. Finally, he gave a disgusted shrug, started his horse, and took after Grissom.

The old-timer was grinning vacantly again, lips pinched in over toothless gums. Stallcup glared at him. "You, too, Amos," he said.

"He-he," said the old-timer, and wheeled his horse, racing off at a breakneck gallop.

Gatewood began mopping the sweat off his face and

neck. Stallcup watched him with a faint amusement.

"If you can stand a drink, Gatewood, come with me."

The place was a combined trading post, general store, and saloon, set down lonely and desolate here deep in the Doloritas. There was just this one building, situated at the base of a high, rearing rampart of reddish-brown stone. Gatewood wondered that anyone would want to build in such an out-of-the-way, impractical place like this, but he supposed there was traffic of a sort from isolated ranchers and trappers.

The place was one big room, with mountain lion hides stacked in one corner, canned goods and ammunition and traps and bait all piled together in confusion in the center, and a short, cedar-plank bar along the other wall. The owner was a short, fat man in greasy clothing who answered to the name of Hilary.

Stallcup asked for his private bottle and winked at Gatewood. Hilary made a face and came up with a gallon of corn whiskey from under the bar, slamming it down with an irritated gesture that plainly said this was all he served, and they could drink it and like it or go somewhere else.

Stallcup filled two tin cups and shoved one at Gatewood. Then, with a great gulp, Stallcup drained half his cup. He wheezed mightily while tears brimmed his eyes, and then he smiled and said: "Damn, that's good."

Gatewood took a small sip of his drink, feeling it burn a path all the way down to his stomach, but, after a moment, it changed to a mellow, comforting glow. Stallcup now drained the rest of his liquor, then filled his cup again. He held the jug half tilted and looked inquiringly at Gatewood.

"You're falling behind," said Stallcup.

Gatewood held a hand over his cup. "I've just been

weaned from temperance," he said. "I'm not used very much to the stuff yet."

"Suit yourself," said Stallcup, putting down the jug. He peered narrowly at Gatewood. "How come you ever went to work for the Association?"

"What's wrong with the Association?"

"I didn't say there's anything wrong with it," said Stallcup. "I'm just curious how come you're doing this kind of work, instead of punching cows or something like that?"

Gatewood paused a moment before answering. This was a question he had been asking himself with increasing frequency of late. He remembered all the jobs he had been on and the things, some of them unpleasant, that he had seen, and he knew again the urge to quit.

"Maybe it's the pay," he said musingly. "Or maybe it's because I'm really a drifter at heart. Working for the Association, I go here and I go there. I'm always on the move, yet I've always got some pay coming. To tell you the truth, Stallcup, I really don't know. I went to work for the Association one day, and I'm still with it after five years."

"Well, every man to his taste," said Stallcup, raising his drink. This time he drained the cup with one swallow, drawing the back of his hand over his mouth when he was done and sighing with pleasure.

Gatewood kept remembering what had happened a short while ago. He recalled how quickly Grissom and Daniels and Clark had succumbed to Stallcup's commands, and this remembrance brought a little sadness to Gatewood. He could not help liking Stallcup.

"I don't believe I've thanked you yet for what you did back there, Stallcup," Gatewood said slowly. "Why did you do it?"

"I just paid you back what I owed you. Now my conscience is clear. We start all over again, with neither of us owing the other anything." Stallcup suddenly reached over and clapped Gatewood on the back. "Forget it, *amigo,*" he said. "Why worry about anything until you come face to face with it? Who knows, the job might be too much for you, anyhow. Let's have one more drink."

Gatewood again declined having his cup re-filled. Stallcup shrugged, filled his tin cup until the liquor sloshed over onto the bar, and then tossed it off like it was a drink of water. He burped once after it was down, then licked his lips. With a nod of his head he beckoned to Gatewood, and they went outside.

The woman was waiting beside the roan and the mare. Her pinto was drinking out of the trough in front of the store, indicating that she must have just arrived. She gave a quick look at Stallcup, taking in his flushed features, then her eyes moved and rested on Gatewood.

She was slim and dark and very attractive. Her hair was raven black and hung down loosely, touching her shoulders. Her eyes were a deep, warm brown, and her skin had been burned by the sun until it was the color of smoked leather. Her nose was turned up at the tip, and her lips were long and thin, and there was a cleft in her chin.

Her eyes caught Gatewood's and remained a moment locked like that. Then, casually, they returned to Stallcup. She said: "At it again, Wade?"

A look of hurt innocence came over Stallcup's face. "Just a nip, Dorcas," he said. "Why, I hardly wet my lips."

Her eyes came back to Gatewood. He found he could not keep his glance off her. There was something strangely compelling about her. Perhaps it was the hint of a long, old sadness that showed in the grave lines around her mouth.

Stallcup noticed her interest in Gatewood. "Uh, this is

Gatewood, Dorcas," he said. "He's an inspector for the Cattle Growers Association. Gatewood, this is Dorcas Renshaw."

IV

Since this part of it had proved fruitless, Gatewood decided to go at it from the other end. If the rustlers were running stolen Stirrup beef into Mexico, Gatewood thought he'd try to find out where they crossed the border and then work back into the Doloritas on the off chance of running into the rustlers' hide-out in that manner.

Thus it was that Gatewood came upon the cañon. It wound its immense, serpentine way northward into the Doloritas, and Gatewood rode up this to see where it led. All about, the mountains reared barren and sterile. The walls of the cañon sloped upward to great heights where they merged into ragged crests.

The land seemed dead. There was no sign of life. The only vegetation was a bunch of sagebrush here and there and an occasional clump of mesquite. A sense of malignancy, a feeling of ugly, vicious brooding seemed to permeate the air. The mare's hoofs made soft whispers of sound as it moved up the cañon floor.

Gatewood felt his nerves get on edge. He was accustomed to solitude, to exploring lonely, desolate places, but something told him that there was more to this than the apparent emptiness of the land. He began searching the heights of the cañon walls with apprehensive eyes.

It was during one of these uneasy glances upward that he spotted the faint flash close to the cañon's rim. So quick and brief was the thing that he was tempted to pass it off as an illusion, but in his years with the Association Gatewood had learned to take nothing lightly. So it was that, when he heard the whine of the bullet pass his ear, he was going down out of the saddle and hitting the ground even before the sound of the shot came drifting down to the floor of the cañon.

As he left the saddle, Gatewood had yanked his Winchester from its saddle scabbard, and, holding the gun, he raced ahead to the dubious shelter of a clump of mesquite. The gun up on the cañon wall let fly again, this bullet kicking up dirt a foot to the left of Gatewood as he threw himself flat on the ground behind the mesquite.

He lay there, breath coming fast, sweat starting to trickle down his cheeks, wetting the whiskers on his face. A bullet came whistling through the mesquite just over Gatewood's back, and he knew he had to get out of there fast. A clump of mesquite wasn't exactly bulletproof, he thought grimly, and whoever it was up on the cañon wall could keep on pouring slugs into the mesquite until one or more found its mark.

Off to Gatewood's right were several large slabs of rock. He gathered himself up on his knees, sucked in his breath, and lit out at a crouching run. The gun up on the cañon wall let out three fast shots. One of them burned a small gash along Gatewood's arm, but then he was flat on his belly amid the rocks, listening to two more bullets chipping bits off the boulders.

Then the silence settled down. Whoever it was up on the rim must have decided to wait Gatewood out, instead of wasting any more shells. The sun burned down on Gatewood. He had no water. His canteen was on his saddle on the mare's back. He could only crouch there among the rocks, feeling the sun and waiting for the thirst to begin.

It was not long in coming. First his throat dried out, and then his tongue, and after that his lips grew brittle and began to crack. About every fifteen minutes the gunman up on the rim would let go with a single shot just to let Gatewood know he was still there.

Once, in the grip of rage, Gatewood shoved his Winchester above a rock and levered six fast shots up at the cañon wall. When Gatewood was through, the gunman waited a minute, then sent one mocking shot down over the rocks. Gatewood buried his face against the sand while virulent curses gritted through his clenched teeth.

Then he forced the wrath and the needling irritation from him and began to wait as calmly as he could, grimly determined to make the best of it. Every now and then he would peer over the rocks to make sure that no one was sneaking up on him. He threw no more wild shots, even though the gunman, at regularly spaced intervals, sent a slug whining over Gatewood's rocks.

The sun was at its highest and hottest, and the thirst was really beginning to torment Gatewood when he heard the flurry of shots. His first instinct was to crouch lower below the shelter of his boulders, but then he realized that these shots weren't meant for him. Cautiously he glanced up the cañon wall, and far above he saw a man come out from behind a parapet of rock and go streaking over the rim, carrying his rifle with him. This apparently was the bushwhacker, and Gatewood, although he knew he had little chance of hitting anything, threw two shots at the fleeing man. By this time the fellow had topped the rim and was gone from sight.

After a while, the rider showed, coming down the sloping wall of the cañon. There seemed to be no hostile intent about this horseman, so Gatewood came out of his rocks and hurried over to where his mare was waiting with trailing reins, nibbling half-heartedly at a mesquite. Grabbing his canteen, Gatewood satisfied his thirst and then turned his attention to the approaching rider who had by now reached the cañon floor.

The rider was Dorcas Renshaw.

She halted her pinto and stared gravely at Gatewood a while. Finally she dismounted and walked up to him. She was wearing a wide-brimmed black felt hat, a black and red checkered flannel shirt, and tight-fitting Levi's faded from many washings. At her right hip she wore an ivory-handled .41 Colt Lightning pistol.

Gatewood felt his throat tighten a little as he stared at her. He could not understand what it was about her that moved him so. It wasn't just her beauty; it was more that hint of latent sadness that showed hauntingly in her eyes.

He felt awkward and ill at ease and not a little ashamed to have had a woman get him out of his tight. "Well, thanks," he mumbled.

She let it pass without comment, staring fixedly all the while at Gatewood, seemingly trying to decide something about him.

At last she said: "Why don't you go home, Gatewood? You're not getting anywhere. Go home before you get yourself killed."

"What makes you think I'm not getting anywhere?" he asked acidly. "If I was hopeless, nobody would try to kill me. It's because they're afraid of what I'll do that they want to get rid of me. Besides, I've never been a quitter."

She made an impatient gesture. "No one's calling you a quitter or any other names. I'm telling you this because I've got you tallied as a decent sort. Let the rotten ones pick up lead on this job. Go back home and say this is too big for you and let the Association send someone else."

Gatewood eyed her narrowly. "What's your interest in this?"

"I don't have any interest in anything. It's just that I like you, Gatewood. You're not arrogant or mean just because you're in a position to hurt someone you don't like. You work for Stirrup . . . you work for the big fellows . . . but you're the kind to give a break to everybody. Well, this isn't that kind of a deal. Go on home and tell the Association to send you somewhere else."

"I never yet started a job that I didn't finish," he said. "Why should I make an exception this time? Because *you* asked me?"

She moved in a little closer to him, so near he could smell the scent of woodsmoke in her clothes. "Wouldn't that be enough, Gatewood?" she said huskily. "If I asked you, wouldn't that be enough?"

Perhaps because the first time he had seen her he had wanted to know the feel of her in his arms, he wanted one small taste of something which he suspected might never again be his. He pulled her in against him and pressed his mouth down on hers. She came willingly enough, but there was no warmth in her kiss. Despite her quick compliance he sensed the reluctance that was deep within her.

There was a cloying sadness in him as he released her. He understood now how it was with him. He was sorry that he had let himself go like this. Now it was done and in his heart and a permanent part of him, but it wasn't anything at all like that with her.

The girl stood with bowed head, and even the darkness of her skin could not conceal the flush on her face. "I'm sorry, Gatewood," she said with a small catch in her voice.

She looked shamed and hurt, and a quick sympathy for

her came to Gatewood. He wanted to say something to help her, but the words just would not come to his mind.

"I'm not cheap," she said. "I've had it tough all my life, and I've done certain things I'm not exactly proud of, but I've never been cheap." Her face suddenly lifted, eyes appealing to him. "You don't think I'm cheap, do you? I didn't do it because of that. I like you, but. . . ."

"I understand, Dorcas," he said. Then a sudden thought struck him. His eyes narrowed.

"Renshaw," he murmured. "Are you any relation to Buck Renshaw?"

"He's my father-in-law. I'm a widow, Gatewood. My husband has been dead for over a year."

He could not think of anything to say, and it must have been the same for her. She stood there mutely, eyes downcast, that sadness plain on her face, and now this much was clear for Gatewood. It was the memory of her dead husband that left its grave, mournful shadow in her eyes.

An awkward silence filled in between them. She lifted her eyes once to him, then quickly mounted her pinto, and started down the cañon in the direction Gatewood had come from. He watched her go, hoping that she'd turn once and make some sign of farewell, but she kept staring straight ahead until she was out of sight.

Gatewood sighed, got on his mare, and wearily put his mind on his job again.

V

This search, too, proved fruitless and, since he was low on supplies, Gatewood decided to ride into Stirrup. He did not like the prospect of this very much, but there were some things he wanted to know, and he wouldn't find them out unless he did some asking.

He found a sullen anger mounting in him at the thought of encountering Farrell again. Gatewood was no brawler, although he had never backed down from a fight. Still, he was on a job, and it wasn't exactly good policy to fight with his employers, and he was working for Stirrup, even if he got his pay from the Association. He had taken all he cared to take from Farrell, and it would be extremely difficult to overlook the man's arrogance.

He was relieved, when he discovered that Farrell was not at headquarters. The information Gatewood was interested in would be better obtained from the Renshaws, but he hesitated calling on Buck Renshaw. Remembering the dull sorrow in the man's eyes, Gatewood could not bring himself to talk about it to Renshaw.

Gatewood washed up and shaved, and, while he was doing this, the cook whipped up a good meal for him. Thus feeling refreshed and with most of the edge gone from his temper, he went outside. He saw Ellerine Renshaw mounting a shining palomino down by the corrals. She was wearing a cream-colored Stetson and a white silk shirt and a fancy calf-skin vest and a fringed, divided riding skirt. She looked fresh and wholesome, and Gatewood thought he had never seen a prettier woman.

She noticed him standing just outside the cook shack and came cantering up on the palomino, smiling and saying a little breathlessly: "Hello, there."

Gatewood nodded and smiled in return.

She looked approvingly at his shaved features. "You should shave more often," she said, mildly jibing.

"In the Doloritas you don't exactly have the comforts of home," he observed. "Going riding?"

"Yes?" she said.

"Mind if I join you? There are some things I'd like to know, and we can talk as we ride. Do you have a horse I can use? I've been pushing my mare kind of hard lately, and I'd like her to get a little rest. Tomorrow I'm going back into the Doloritas."

The girl pointed out a blaze-faced chestnut which she said was hers, and Gatewood went into the corral, roped the horse, and saddled it. Then with the girl he rode up the valley.

They rode in silence. Despite his professed intention of talking to the girl, Gatewood could not bring himself to get started. At a point near where the timber began, the girl reined in her palomino. Gatewood halted the chestnut beside her. They were on a hill from where they could look down the length of the valley, seeing all its lushness and the thrust of the buildings of Stirrup off in the distance.

When Gatewood did not speak, the girl said quietly: "You mentioned something about wanting to talk to me."

Gatewood pursed his lips. He had never thought it would be this hard to get started on it. Slowly he said: "I ran into something in the Doloritas."

She gave a quick, eager look at him. "Are you onto the rustlers?"

He smiled ruefully. "I'm afraid it isn't anything like that. I . . . I met a woman. Dorcas Renshaw."

"Oh?" she said, then began staring studiously down the valley.

"Maybe it's none of my business, and I don't like to pry, but I'm a little anxious. Who is she?"

"Didn't she tell you?"

"All she said was that she was a widow. I didn't like to press her for more, so I let it go like that."

The girl went on staring down the valley. "So you thought you'd come and press me for information," she said stiffly.

"All right," he growled, "forget it."

She reached over suddenly and caught his arm. "I'm sorry," she said. "It's hard to talk about. Please try to understand, Gatewood."

Moisture glistened in her eyes, and Gatewood was sorry for having been so abrupt with her. She no longer looked cool and distant. She seemed like a small, bewildered child.

"If it's hard on you," he said gently, "you needn't talk about it."

Her mouth stiffened resolutely. "There's not much to say. Dorcas was married to my brother, Jim. Dad and Jim just didn't get along, and Jim moved out. He tried running a little place of his own in the Doloritas, but about a year ago he . . . died."

There followed a silence between them. Gatewood had the feeling that there was more to it than what the girl had just said. The pain and dejection ran too deeply in Renshaw and Dorcas to pass it off with such a simple explanation. But Gatewood did not like probing into it any further. This wasn't his job. His job was to track down the rustlers stealing Stirrup beef. Family problems were not in his line of work.

He became conscious of the girl's eyes, staring at him with a studied speculation. "Why did you ask about Dorcas?"

Gatewood shrugged. "I was just curious. She said her name was Renshaw, and I wanted to know what relation, if any, she was to you and your father."

The girl began fiddling with her palomino's ears. "Dorcas is all right," she said. "I always got along with her.

Dad is different. He had his heart set on Jim's marrying the daughter of an old friend, but Jim wanted Dorcas. Jim always was independent. He had his ideas about how Stirrup should be run, but Dad couldn't see it Jim's way. It was a lot of little things building up, and Jim finally got fed up and left."

There was something about her which he could not quite grasp, a feeling that she was forcibly holding herself in. "Is there anything else you want to tell me, anything about Stirrup . . . about you?"

Her lower lip began to tremble. Her eyes moistened, and suddenly all the pent-up fury in her burst out in a hoarse, ferine growl. "I hate Stirrup! I hate the land. I hate the people. I hate everything that keeps me tied down here. I hate it . . . I hate it . . . I hate it!"

He held her against him, and after a while her sobs stilled. She lifted her head and pulled away from him. She wiped her eyes and face with a handkerchief and then said, her voice perceptibly under control: "I'm sorry for being such a crybaby, Gatewood. Well, should we start back to Stirrup?"

That evening Gatewood had just joined in a game of pitch with three of the Stirrup riders in the bunkhouse when Farrell called him outside. Farrell walked over to a corral, and Gatewood followed, an unpleasant premonition stirring inside him.

Farrell finally halted, and the reason for it became apparent to Gatewood. They were out of earshot of the bunkhouse here. Farrell went about rolling a smoke with a slow preoccupation and at last put it in his mouth. He scratched a match with his thumb and lit his cigarette. In the glow of the matchlight his face looked saturnine and grim.

"Gatewood," he said, "what do your duties consist of as an inspector for the Cattle Association?"

"I don't get you, Farrell."

"Is romancing a part of your job?"

An ugly resentment moved in Gatewood. He could sense more unpleasantness coming, more frayed temper.

"If it's what I think you mean, I don't like it," he said grimly.

"Let me put you straight, Gatewood. Stirrup is a mighty valuable piece of property, and some day it's going to belong to Miss Ellerine. I know it's a tempting thing to certain kinds of people, but no one's gonna make a play for her with the idea of someday coming into Stirrup, least of all a bum of an inspector for the Cattle Growers Association!"

Gatewood's fists clenched. "You're sure going to a lot of pains asking for something," he said through his teeth. "One of these days you're going to get everything you've got coming."

Farrell's smile was a white, jeering grimace. "I can dish it out as well as take it, Gatewood."

"How?" said Gatewood. "By getting two of your flunkies to tie a man to a tree and then whipping him when he's helpless?"

"Don't you needle me. I gave my word to Mister Renshaw that I'd get along with you, but don't you needle me. And I'm warning you to stay away from Miss Ellerine! Have you got that through your thick skull?"

"So you spied," growled Gatewood. "You sneaked around and spied on me."

"Spied?" shouted Farrell. "It was all out in the open for anyone to see! I came through the timber, and I saw you holding her."

Gatewood said, his voice thick with restraint: "I don't

brawl when I'm on a job, Farrell. You don't like me, and I sure as the devil don't like you. Once my job is done, I'll look you up. Remember that. I'm not forgetting this."

"Suits me, Gatewood," said Farrell. "I can hardly wait for you to wind up your job. In fact, I'm going to take a hand in it myself again just to hurry up the finish."

VI

Gatewood went back into the Doloritas. For two more days he searched fruitlessly. Then he came upon the first hopeful sign of his investigation. While traveling up a long, crooked draw that seemed to head right up into the base of a towering peak, he came upon the fresh droppings of a cow and the tracks of two cows and a horse that apparently was driving the cattle.

He got down out of the saddle and examined the marks carefully. This could very well be it. He was deep into the Doloritas here, far beyond the limits of Stirrup, and, if these were Stirrup cattle, then they had been driven all the way up here for they hardly would have strayed this far into rugged, barren, inhospitable country.

Gatewood was still bent over, studying the sign, when he sensed the presence of something behind him. He leaped to his feet and spun around, hand stabbing for the handle of his .44, and then he saw the big bore of a .45 gaping at him and the rock-steady hand holding it.

Lifting his glance, Gatewood looked into the chill, cruel, glittering purpose shining in the fellow's eyes.

The man holding the gun was Amos Clark.

His buckskins were dirtier than ever, it seemed. He emanated an offensive stench. His mouth was cracked open in a vapid grin that did not go at all with the cunning intelligence in his eyes. He had been chewing on tobacco with his toothless gums, and the juice had trickled down out of the corners of his mouth, staining the whiskers on his chin with streaks of filthy brown.

Slowly Gatewood raised his hands without being told to do so. Clark came ahead, moving lithely, soundlessly, on his moccasined feet, and Gatewood now understood how Clark had managed to creep up unobserved. Either he had been following Gatewood, or Clark had been the horseman going up the draw and had become aware of being trailed and so had climbed out of the draw and doubled back.

"Turn around," said Clark.

Gatewood obeyed. Clark closed in, swiftly plucked the .44 out of Gatewood's holster, and stepped back. Gatewood turned, facing Clark again.

Triumph flared in the wide grin on the old man's face. "He-he," he said.

The touch of madness in it brought a chill to the back of Gatewood's neck. He made a swift summation of his chances against Clark's .45 and decided none of them was hopeful. He began to sweat.

"If you know what's good for you, Gatewood, you'll do everything I say," Clark said, wagging his .45.

He made Gatewood get his mare, and then ordered him to climb out of the wash. Clark's horse was up beyond the rim of the wash, tethered to a piñon. Clark had Gatewood mount the mare, and then bound Gatewood's wrists to his saddle horn. Getting on his horse, Clark started away, leading the mare.

Gatewood estimated the ride took about two hours. Finally Clark stopped in front of an old shack set against the base of a high ledge amid a scattering of jackpine. Clark loosed the cord holding Gatewood's wrists to the saddle horn but still left Gatewood's hands bound. He ordered Gatewood into the shack.

Gatewood almost gagged on the stench that filled the place. There was just the one room. A box stove was in the middle of the place. A pile of skins and blankets were in one corner on the floor, and these evidently served as Clark's bed. Clark made Gatewood lie down on these and then, holstering his .45, bound Gatewood's legs.

That done, Clark rose to his feet. His eyes glistened with a vile anticipation that sent a shiver through Gatewood. He was wearing a Bowie knife in a fancy, beaded sheath at his left hip, and now the old man took out the knife and began feeling the keen edge with his thumb. His eyes glared avidly all the while.

"Tell me, Gatewood," he said, "what should I do with you?"

Sweat trickled down into Gatewood's eyes; he could taste the salt of it on his lips. "You could always turn me loose," he said dryly.

"He-he," said Clark. "That's funny. He-he-he. That's the funniest thing I ever heard."

Gatewood's heart was pounding leadenly. "What did I ever do to you, Clark?" he asked. "I've never done you any harm. Wade Stallcup is your friend, isn't he? Well, I helped Stallcup. When Steve Farrell was whipping Stallcup, I set him free. Farrell would have whipped Stallcup to death. Don't you see?"

A crafty gleam came into the old man's eyes. "Ah, no," he said, grinning wider. "He-he-he."

"All right, don't take my word for it. Go get Stallcup. Bring him here and ask him. Let him tell you if we're friends or not."

Old Clark shook his head, grinning all the time. "I'm too

smart for that, Gatewood. I'm not leaving you alone. Why, you're company. I got to stay here and help you pass the time. Now let me see. What could we do that would be some fun?" He cocked his head to one side and pawed at his beard while a cruel glitter came into his eyes. "I know what the Pawnees used to do for fun. When I was a young man, I lived with the Pawnees for three years. I married a Pawnee squaw. I know all about Pawnee ways."

Clark squatted down on his haunches and waved the Bowie in front of Gatewood's face. "Did you know that the Pawnees used to practice human sacrifices, Gatewood? They used to sacrifice them to the Morning Star. I remember one of them. It was in April, at the beginning of the planting season. The Pawnees had a Sioux girl they had taken captive. They fed her well for a time and fattened her up, and all the while she had no idea what was going to happen to her. On that morning she visited every wigwam in the village. With her was the chiefs and all the warriors. At every wigwam she was given a small bit of wood and some paint. She handed these over to the warriors until all of them had two pieces of wood and some paint. Then they took her and painted her body half black and half red. Then they hung her from a gibbet and roasted her a while over a slow fire. Then they shot her to death with arrows. After that, the medicine man cut out her heart and ate it. Then they cut her flesh up into small pieces and carried them out to the cornfield and squeezed drops of blood on the newly planted grains of corn. The Pawnees believed that if they did not make this sacrifice to the Morning Star that nothing would grow, and they would all starve to death. But they also got a lot of fun out of it. How would you like me to sacrifice you to the Morning Star, Gatewood?"

Gatewood could feel the sweat coursing clammily down

his chest beneath his shirt. His throat constricted. He looked into the old man's eyes and realized sickeningly that Clark was deadly serious about it.

"No, I don't think I will," Clark conceded finally. "It's too much bother. But there are other ways I can have some fun. With my Bowie I can have lots of fun."

He lunged suddenly forward, smashing Gatewood down on his back. Gatewood tried to strike up with his bound hands, but Clark jumped on top, pinning his tied wrists to his chest with one knee. The glittering point of the Bowie hovered just above Gatewood's eyes.

Old Clark was drooling with feral anticipation, the wetness dripping off his lower lip onto his beard. "I could cut out your eyes," he said thoughtfully, "one by one. I could cut out your tongue. I could slice off your nose and your ears. You wouldn't die because of that, would you?"

The Bowie poised. With a sick, desperate feeling in his stomach, Gatewood tried to work his bound legs so as to get some leverage for a sudden heave, but he couldn't get anywhere with the old man's weight on him.

"He-he," said Clark, and started down with the knife.

The shot rang out, the concussion seeming to shake the walls of the shack. Clark gave a small, startled scream and jumped to his feet, the Bowie clattering to the floor. Sweat streaming down his face, Gatewood lifted himself up to a sitting position so that he could see.

In the doorway, .41 smoking in her hand, was Dorcas Renshaw.

Her narrowed eyes blazed. "I should kill you, Amos," she snarled. "You know that, don't you? You're sick, and before you're through you're going to do something awful. The only way to stop that is to kill you."

The old man spread his hands in a plaintive gesture. "I

was only having a little fun," he said whiningly.

"I saw you, and you meant everything you said, Amos."

"No, no!" he cried. "I was just funning. Honest I was, Dorcas."

Some of the rage passed from her, and she relented a little. "All right," she said. "Throw Gatewood's gun to the floor and then get out of here. Get out and keep riding and don't stop until you're miles away from here. And don't ever again let me catch you trying a thing like this again. If I do, so help me, Amos, I'll shoot you down without a word."

After the old man had gone, Dorcas picked up the Bowie and cut Gatewood's bonds. He hesitated getting to his feet, for he did not know if he could make it, all the muscles of his body were so weak and fluttery. But he managed it all right.

He glanced ruefully at Dorcas. "This is getting to be a habit for you."

"Let's get out of here," she said. "I don't see how you can stand the stink."

Outside, Gatewood breathed deeply of the clean air. He had taken his .44 out with him and then shoved the weapon in his holster. Dorcas was standing by her pinto, watching him gravely.

Some of her somberness worked into him, and suddenly he could think only of what she meant to him and of all the implications of her presence here. He walked up to her and cupped her chin in his hand and lifted her face and stared down at her a while. She looked right back at him, never averting her eyes.

"Dorcas," he said softly, "where do you fit into all this?"

"Fit into what?"

"You know what. My job here . . . Stallcup . . . Clark. . . . Grissom. . . . Daniels?"

Abruptly she freed her chin and turned her back to him. Her voice came low and muffled. "I don't fit in anywhere. I live here in the Doloritas. As for Wade Stallcup and the others, they're good friends of mine. What they happen to be doing is no concern of mine. They don't ask me any questions, and I don't ask them any."

He put a hand to her shoulder. "Listen to me, Dorcas," he said. "I've got a job to do. I don't want you hurt in doing it."

She turned and smiled up at him. "Hurt me? Don't be silly. How could you possibly hurt me?"

He felt miserable and mean inside. He had a feeling that this job did not have much longer to go, and, the way things looked to him now, he could only see pain and heartbreak ahead for him. He closed his fingers tightly about her shoulder, and she winced. He eased up a little and said: "Let's not kid ourselves any more. You know how it is without my putting it into so many words."

A pleading earnestness showed in her eyes. "You've got to quit," she cried tensely, clutching his arms with her fingers. "You'll be killed, if you don't. Can't you just say this job is too much for you and let the Association send another man? I . . . I wouldn't want to come across your dead body someday here in the Doloritas. You mean too much to me, Gatewood."

He could feel it all stirring inside him again, the yearning for her, the need for her. Never in his life had any woman moved him as much as this one did.

He put his arms around her and pulled her close and tight, feeling the fierce, eager warmth of her against him, his mouth bruising down on hers. She tried to respond, but he could feel the reluctance in her, and suddenly she wasn't trying any more but was just standing there passively in his arms.

Sadly, he released her, comprehending a little how things were and how they would be and wishing fiercely that they could be otherwise. She stared wide-eyed and hurt, as if she regretted it as much as he did.

"I do love you," she whispered. "I want you so much to know that. I'm not trying to buy you off. This isn't any job for you. It's a mean and vicious and dirty thing, and you shouldn't have any part of it. Please, Gatewood. Please tell me you'll give this up. Tell me that, and then kiss me again. . . ."

VII

The land here was rugged, full of primordial upheavals and weird, eroded shapes that left their mark in steep slopes and precipitous heights. Monstrous fragments of rock littered the ground, and among these the small creek wriggled and flashed. Gatewood halted the mare to allow it to drink, and he dismounted and drank himself of the cold, rushing water. This was the best-tasting water he had encountered here in the Doloritas, and he drank deeply.

From where he stood the ground fell away rather sharply, and, according to the information he had been given, Gatewood figured he was just about at the northern limits of Stirrup. He looked down to where the ground leveled out below him, fanning out into a small plain surrounded by hills. Here, too, vegetation was stunted and sparse.

Something moved slightly beneath a tall cedar, and Gatewood shaded his eyes with his hands and peered more intently. He still could not see clearly, for the tree was far enough away, but he did not need a close-up look to know what it was that had caught his eyes. Hurriedly he mounted the mare and sent it at a run down the slope.

The dead man swung by his neck from the lowest branch of the cedar. There was a small wind, and he swayed gently in it, swinging to and fro with a quiet, chilling rhythm. The dead man was Lonnie Grissom.

Gatewood raised a fist and brandished it mutely, futilely. Then with the rage mounting through him, he went to work. He cut down Grissom's body, dumped it in a small hollow, and covered it with stones. Then Gatewood mounted his mare and headed for Stirrup.

Coming down the north end of the valley, Gatewood spied the horseman ahead of him, apparently with the intention of going into the timber. Recognition came instantly, and he whipped the mare into a swift run. The rider, Steve Farrell, heard the drumming of the mare's hoofs and whipped around in his saddle. When he saw that it was Gatewood, Farrell reined in his buckskin and waited.

Gatewood brought the mare to a sliding halt. He leaped to the ground, chest heaving with anger. "Get off your horse," he snarled.

Farrell stayed in his saddle.

"You yellow-bellied son-of-a-bitch!" Gatewood shouted. "Get off your horse before I drag you off!"

Farrell's face diffused with rage. "I'll teach you to talk to me like that," he said through his teeth. He whirled the buckskin around, aimed it at Gatewood, and jabbed the horse with the spurs.

Gatewood whipped out his .44, pointing it at Farrell with the hammer eared back. Gatewood's finger was tight on the trigger.

"You try to run me down, Farrell, and I'll blow you right out of your kak. Now get down. You hear?"

With Gatewood's .44 out, Farrell reined in the buckskin

so sharply the animal reared high, front legs thrashing, almost going over backwards. With a hard pull on the reins, Farrell brought the horse down and hipped around in the saddle to glare at Gatewood.

"I found Grissom," said Gatewood.

A cruel, triumphant smile crossed Farrell's mouth. "So that's what you're so hot about. Well, that's one less rustler to worry about. I told you I was taking a hand, and, when I take a hand, I get results."

Gatewood still pointed the .44. "Did you catch Grissom in the act? If you did, why didn't you turn him over to the law for prosecution? You think you're the law, Farrell?"

"You're god-damn' right I'm the law," Farrell shouted, pounding his chest with a fist. "On Stirrup I'm the law. I'm Stirrup, you hear? Me . . . Steve Farrell . . . I'm Stirrup. Not Renshaw, not that stupid daughter of his, not anyone but me, Steve Farrell. You think I'm gonna sit around on my rump while these rustlers keep on running off Stirrup stock and you go picking daisies in the Doloritas? I'll show you how to stop that rustling, Gatewood. Grissom was only the start. I left him swinging as a warning to the others. If they don't take that warning, they're next on the program. Stallcup, Daniels, and Clark. They'll all swing from a tree in the Doloritas, if Stirrup keeps on losing stock."

"Just like that, eh?" said Gatewood. "Listen, Farrell, I'm not trying to defend anybody, but every man has a right to a fair trial. I won't coddle anybody. When I catch those rustlers . . . and I am going to catch them . . . I'll see that they get a break. If they choose to make a fight of it, I'll kill them, but not before I give them a chance.

"One more thing. I told you once that I'd wait until my job was over before calling you on some of the things you've done and said. Well, I've changed my mind. I'm calling you now. Get off that horse and take off your gun belt, if you aren't too yellow."

"I'll show you how yellow I am!" Farrell cried. He leaped from the saddle, unbuckled his shell belt, and flung it viciously to the ground. Then he waited while Gatewood did the same.

Farrell advanced with arms spread wide as if with the intention of grasping and crushing Gatewood in a powerful embrace. Farrell's face was twisted, his mouth pulled down at the corners, the cords in his neck standing out. He came on, and, as Gatewood moved in to drive a blow at Farrell's middle, Farrell suddenly shifted, slipping to Gatewood's left and lashing out with a boot.

The blow caught Gatewood on the thigh. It was vicious enough to send him staggering. As Farrell saw this, he closed in with a virulent shout. Again he kicked out, aiming at Gatewood's groin, but Gatewood had been expecting something like this, and he jumped back, just barely avoiding the kick. As it was, his feet slipped, and he went sprawling.

Farrell shouted again, in triumph this time, and lunged in, right boot lifting to stomp down in Gatewood's face. Desperately, Gatewood caught the foot as it was coming down. He twisted his head, getting it out of the way as the boot crashed down, just missing him. Even so, the sharp spur on the heel drove into Gatewood's shoulder, and a sear of pain flashed across his mind.

But he had a hold on Farrell's leg and would not let go. With sweat streaming down his face, he rolled to the side, tugging mightily at Farrell's leg. The man squalled in alarm as he felt his balance waver, and then he came crashing down beside Gatewood.

As Farrell hit the ground, Gatewood twisted and dove on

the man. Farrell started to come up, and Gatewood smashed him in the mouth. The rage had enveloped all of Gatewood now. He sobbed with it. Farrell tried to reach up and grab Gatewood's neck, and Gatewood smashed him on the cheek.

Farrell's lips were raw and bleeding. He spat blood, and then with an immense heave he twisted and squirmed and kicked out, raking a spur down Gatewood's back. Gatewood moaned with the pain of it. He tried to keep from going off Farrell, but the man gave another heave, and Gatewood went rolling.

He jumped to his feet to find Farrell rushing at him. The man came on with a wild, furious charge, head lowered. He bulled through a terrific swing by Gatewood and smashed his head into Gatewood's middle. The breath whooshed out of Gatewood. Sickness swept him nauseatingly. For a moment he felt all strength desert him, and he fell to the ground, Farrell on top of him.

The man was cursing in fury. He brought up a knee viciously for Gatewood's groin, but Gatewood blocked it with a sudden, mighty squirm. Then Farrell's hands were on Gatewood's face, digging, gouging, seeking Gatewood's eyes. Gatewood got two fistfuls of Farrell's hair and yanked. Gatewood kept on pulling with all his strength, and suddenly the ramrod began to scream with anguish. His hands began clawing frantically at Gatewood's wrists in a desperate attempt to break his hold.

Gatewood let go with his right hand and swiftly smashed it up against Farrell's mouth. With his left hand still clutching Farrell's hair, Gatewood began raining short, vicious blows into the ramrod's face. Farrell began to moan with agony. He tried reaching for Gatewood's eyes again, but Gatewood smashed the hands away and drove more blows into Farrell's face. Now Farrell tried covering up with both arms. Gatewood gave a sudden, vicious twist with the hand that grasped Farrell's hair, and, as the man screamed and his arms fell away from his face, Gatewood drove a blow against Farrell's jaw.

Farrell went slack and started to come down limply on Gatewood. Gatewood pushed the ramrod off onto the ground. Farrell was making weak, fumbling efforts to get up. Sobbing with wrath, Gatewood reached down and lifted Farrell up by his shirt front. Then he landed one more blow with all the strength he possessed on Farrell's jaw, and this time, when Farrell hit the ground, he did not move.

Gatewood rose weakly to his feet. His knees kept wanting to give way, and it was only with the greatest effort that he stayed on his feet. He went over and picked up his shell belt and .44 and buckled them on. Then he returned to where Farrell was still out cold on the ground.

"Hang a man without giving him a break, will you?" said Gatewood, and then he spat down into Farrell's face.

VIII

Two days later Gatewood finally found the rustlers' hideout. It was at the end of what apparently was a box cañon. Gatewood had ridden into this, and, when he reached what appeared to be its blank, impenetrable end, he made a close study of it. He was all set to ride off when he saw something that deterred him.

Scrub pine grew all along the lower half of the box end, making a solid wall of green. It was the few trees in the middle of this greenness that were beginning to show signs of drying up that finally caught Gatewood's eye. Some of the needles were just starting to turn brown at the tip. Gatewood rode in closer to investigate and that was how he found the cave.

The entrance was just wide enough to admit a horse or a cow. To conceal the opening, several trees had been hung from ropes tied to other pines above. So cleverly was the job done that, unless a man were immediately on top of the suspended trees, he would have believed that this was all a solid wall with no break whatever in it.

The hole was not high enough to allow a horseman to enter. Gatewood had to dismount and lead the mare into the cave. Inside, the aperture widened somewhat, and some distance ahead Gatewood could see a faint light which he gathered to be the other end of the tunnel. The air in the cave was fetid with the stench of cow dung which was evidence enough that many cattle had passed through here.

The tunnel opened on a small, oblong basin that was like a bit of paradise among the barrenness of the Doloritas. High, rugged crests rimmed the basin, making it inaccessible any way but through the cave. The basin was lush and green with graze, and the slopes all around were thick with timber.

Gatewood emerged cautiously from the cave. There was the possibility that the tunnel was guarded, but this did not seem to be the case. Gatewood figured that the rustlers were so confident their secret was beyond discovery they did not feel it necessary to keep the entrance under constant surveillance.

He could see a number of white-faces grazing close by, and they all wore the Stirrup brand. All through the basin the brown specks of grazing Herefords showed. Gatewood did not want to take the chance of being spotted, so he quickly mounted the mare and sent her up a slope into the cover of the timber.

Here among the concealing pines he made a slow and studied tour all around the basin. It took him quite some time, but he wanted to get a clear picture in his mind of what lay in the basin.

Gatewood was unable to spot any riders. The basin looked deserted except for the cattle. He had spotted the small tarpaper shack set up on the side of a slope just below the ragged line of the timber, and now he came in behind the shack.

He left the mare in the timber, tied to a pine. Then Gatewood moved carefully in. All about him was an awesome, solemn silence. There was an air of placidity, of peace about everything. He walked in slowly, listening to the whisper of the grass brushing against his boots.

He had just reached the back of the shack when Stallcup showed suddenly. Both men spotted each other in the same instant. Stallcup looked just as startled as Gatewood felt. Stallcup was bareheaded, his hair all tousled up, his eyes heavy-lidded as if he had just roused from a deep sleep. In his left hand was an empty pail as if he were on the way to get some water. Now he released the pail and let it clatter to the ground.

Neither man said anything. To Gatewood it was clear enough without putting it into words. There was in Stallcup now none of the easy-going carelessness that he had displayed on other occasions. He was all grim business. It showed in the gelid glint in his eyes, in the tight twist of his lips. His manner indicated plainly that the time for friendliness was gone. All that had happened before, the amiable talk, the pleasant joshing, the sociable drinks — all that was a thing of the past.

Stallcup took a deep breath, and then went for his gun. He brought the Remington .44-40 flashing up as Gatewood's Colt cleared its holster. Gatewood fired. He saw flame spurt out of the Remington and heard the vicious whine of the slug past his ear.

Stallcup was wavering, swaying on his feet. He took another deep breath, while his face strained with pain, and started to bring the Remington up again. Once more Gatewood fired. This time Stallcup emitted a choked cry and dropped abruptly on his face.

He lay on the ground with the Remington just beyond the reach of his outstretched fingers. Gatewood came in carefully and kicked the .44-40 out of reach. Then he knelt beside Stallcup. Gently, Gatewood rolled the man over. Stallcup still lived, although the pallor of death tinged his features.

Gatewood felt the regret come sweeping over him. He had liked Stallcup, he had formed a genuine affection for the man, and now he had had to kill him. Silently, Gatewood began to curse his job.

Stallcup opened his eyes. "No hard feelings, Gatewood?" he asked weakly.

"Why should I have hard feelings?" asked Gatewood, a tightness in his throat. "You should be the one to have them."

Stallcup still smiled. "What the devil," he said. "Why feel bad about it? We just happened to be on opposite sides. It was either you or me. Why should I cry because you got me? I wouldn't have cried over you."

"Sure," said Gatewood. "Why cry about it?"

With fingers that trembled a trifle, Gatewood built a smoke and stuck it in Stallcup's mouth. Gatewood lit the smoke, and Stallcup inhaled deeply and then began to cough in a harsh, convulsive way that brought blood to his lips. But the spasm passed, and he held the smoke up in front of his eyes and gazed at it wistfully and longingly. Then he tossed it away.

"Can't even have that," he mumbled forlornly.

Gatewood could not speak past the cloying tightness in his throat.

Now Stallcup seemed to draw within himself. He sensed the swift, inexorable approach of death, and it seemed that in these last few seconds he wanted to be alone with some secret, cherished remembrances. He lay there with that far-away, pensive look in his eyes, and whatever he was thinking of must have been good and pleasant to him for a small smile came to his lips, and he was like that when death claimed him.

IX

Gatewood reasoned that the best way of catching the remaining rustlers would be to wait for them at the entrance to the basin. Since the cave was so well concealed, no one but the rustlers would be using it, and use of it alone should be proof enough of their complicity.

He had no idea how long he would have to remain here. Perhaps the other rustlers would come this day or night, perhaps within the next hour. Or they might not show up for several days. Then, again, they might straggle in singly, instead of coming in a bunch.

He picketed the mare up in the trees where she was out of sight. Then Gatewood took his Winchester and went down to the entrance to the basin. He selected an outcropping of rock close to the mouth of the cave. This would conceal him from the view of anyone coming into the basin and would also give him an opportunity to get the drop on whoever it was riding into the basin. Gatewood wanted to take the remaining rustlers alive, if he could.

Night closed in over the basin, and still no one came. Gatewood chewed on some jerky and limited his supper to that. He did not want to light a fire. He lay with his back on the grass next to the rock and looked up at the stars.

Gatewood tried to keep the waiting from getting on his nerves. He tried to close his mind to the flood of reminiscences that kept pressing down, but they were too insistent. Everything he had seen and done since he had come to the Doloritas paraded before his mind. He saw the faces of Renshaw, Farrell, Stallcup, Clark, Daniels, Grissom, Ellerine, and Dorcas. Dorcas . . . ?

He felt the tightness come to his throat as he thought of her. In all his life he had never met a woman that had meant anything to him until he met Dorcas. He tried to figure out what it was about her that moved him so strongly, while all other women had been meaningless to him. But he could not pin anything down definitely.

He thought it strange that he kept thinking now and then of Ellerine Renshaw. He reasoned that here it was pity for the girl that stirred him. She had been so miserable and heartbroken that day he had held her in his arms that he could not help but feel sympathy for her. He was just beginning to comprehend some of the things she must have gone through with a grief-stricken father and Farrell's jealous arrogance. Farrell. Gatewood's teeth gritted and regret came that he had not killed Farrell, instead of beating him up. Gatewood's mind worked thus, but always his thoughts reverted to Dorcas.

Gatewood finally dozed a while, and then awoke with a

start. The moon had come up, flooding the basin with a cold, pale light. He groped for his Winchester and pulled it close to him, all the while listening. He was positive that it was some slight, alien sound that had wakened him, but, although he strained his ears, no further noise came.

He rose to his feet and crouched against the concealing rock, listening intently. Sweat stood out on his brow and began to trickle down into his eyes. Angrily, he brushed it away, but it kept popping out on his forehead.

He was about convinced that it was his imagination when the noise came again, and this time there was no doubt that it was real. The sound emanated from within the tunnel. The muted sound of a horse's shod hoof struck a stone.

Gatewood froze with the breath catching a moment in his throat. His mind went swiftly over possibilities. He was tempted to use the Winchester, but whoever it was would pass right in front of the rock and in more than adequate six-shooter range. So Gatewood drew his .44, although he still hung onto the Winchester with his left hand.

Now it became apparent from the nearing sounds that it was more than one man and a horse approaching. Gatewood felt his heart beat faster. This was a stroke of luck. If he could nab both Daniels and Clark, the job would be over for him, and he could get away from the Doloritas and the things that disturbed him so.

The men came on, chattering quietly among themselves as they emerged from the mouth of the tunnel. They rode their horses casually and unhurriedly once they were in the basin and came ahead at a slow walk. It was then that Gatewood noticed there were three of them.

One said something quietly, and then all three laughed together, old Clark's titter sounding high-pitched and eerie.

Gatewood crouched in the shelter of his rock. In the moonlight he recognized them as they passed directly in front of him. If they had looked down and to the side, they would have seen him, but they didn't. They moved easily on — Red Daniels, Amos Clark, and Dorcas.

Gatewood waited until they had passed his rock, and then he stepped out, putting himself between them and the cave. He was chilled inside and angry and hurt. His throat felt clogged, and he feared that he could not speak, but then his voice came, thick and cold.

"Pull up, buckos. Raise your hands and turn your horses slow. I mean business!"

For a moment the three froze, reining in their mounts in startled surprise. They looked inquiringly at each other and seemed to reach some silent, mutual agreement for suddenly all three whirled their horses on Gatewood. He saw them reach for their guns.

With his first slug he knocked Daniels out of the saddle. The second slug Gatewood threw into old Clark. The man gave a choked scream and folded over the saddle horn. His horse gave a wild lunge as the pressure on the lines relaxed, and Clark went pitching to the ground.

Then Gatewood turned on Dorcas.

She had her pinto bearing down on him. The gun in her hand lifted and pointed at him. He could see the set, determined purpose in her strained face. He had his .44 ready, the hammer racked back, the seven-and-a-half inch barrel lined up with her heart.

An inarticulate, wrenching anguish twisted Gatewood's heart, for he realized that he could never go through with it. Even if it meant that she'd kill him, he could not fire at her.

The .44 lowered in Gatewood's hand.

He stood there dully, waiting for the shock of the bullet

tearing into his flesh as Dorcas flashed by him on her pinto. But the same thing must have passed through her mind. At the last instant, her .41 tilted upward, and the slug went screaming off above Gatewood's head. He saw the pale blob of her face, looking back at him over her shoulder, and then she had flattened herself along the pinto's neck as the horse raced into the tunnel.

Gatewood listened until the last sounds of her going had vanished. Then, with the .44 still in his right hand and the Winchester in his left, he examined the men lying on the ground. Daniels was dead. Gatewood turned the man over with the toe of a boot, and Daniels flopped limply, lifelessly on his back. Then Gatewood turned on the sprawled body of old Clark.

Clark lay hunched up in a tightly constricted ball, his face against the ground. Gatewood was just starting to bend over the old fellow when a sudden, chill prescience warned him. Even as he was straightening and dropping back a step, Clark's head lifted abruptly and his hand, holding a tiny Derringer, flung up. Gatewood fired. Clark screamed in animal anguish, but he would not yield. He hunched up on one elbow, the Derringer still lifted.

Gatewood fired again. The slug caught Clark between the eyes. His mouth slacked open, and he dropped suddenly, and now there were two dead man lying on the ground.

X

Gatewood built a fire and cooked himself a meal, but found that he could not eat anything. There was no taste to what he put in his mouth, and he gagged, when he tried to swallow.

But he was able to drink a little coffee.

Then he set about lifting the dead men on their horses and tying them across their saddles. He took his time about it. He did not want to meet Dorcas again, when he left for Stirrup.

Now that he had had a little time to think about it, Gatewood had come to feel that everything had worked out for the best. He regretted having had to kill Stallcup, Clark, and Daniels, but with them dead there was no one to implicate Dorcas with the rustling. As for himself, Gatewood determined not to mention a word about her, no matter how much his conscience might be troubled. After all, the rustling gang was broken up. Dorcas couldn't very well do much by herself.

Gatewood finally moved out of the basin. He had to lead the horses with their dead burdens through the tunnel, one by one. It was dawn, when he reached the mouth of the cañon. An immense stillness seemed to pervade the land. A feeling of forlornness, of heartaching emptiness, crept over Gatewood, and he could not shake his depression. Just beyond the mouth of the cañon Gatewood came upon the body.

It was sprawled behind a large clump of mesquite, and he would have passed it by had he not looked down at this moment. It was as if a constricting hand were closing about Gatewood's throat. He leaped out of the saddle and dropped to his knees beside the still form.

It was Dorcas Renshaw.

He touched her and was wildly hopeful, when he felt warmth still in her. Fumblingly, he felt for her pulse, and it still beat, although faintly. Gently, he turned her over on her back. The front of her shirt was covered with blood from the wound in her chest.

Gatewood took the canteen off his saddle. Then he cradled Dorcas's shoulders in his left arm and forced a little water in her mouth. She swallowed weakly.

Pain wrenched at Gatewood's heart as he stared at her. Her face was pale, her lips colorless. A brief examination of her wound told him that she did not have long to live. Tears stung Gatewood's eyes. An immense rage against whoever had done this swelled in his chest.

Her eyes fluttered a little, and he thought they would open, but they remained closed. "Dorcas," he said, his voice thick with grief, "Dorcas."

This time her eyes opened. She stared blankly, straight upward, as if she did not see him. He spoke her name again, and now the focus of her eyes shifted, and she looked up at him, her face very pale and grave and full of pain.

"Oh, Gatewood, it's you," she whispered. "I'm so glad it's you."

Gatewood's lips trembled. "Who did it, Dorcas?" he asked hoarsely. "Who?"

"Steve Farrell."

Gatewood was stunned. "But why?" he cried. "Why?"

"Because I tried to kill him, but I wasn't up to it. He beat me to it."

He shook his head dumbly. "I don't understand, Dorcas."

She reached up a weak hand and touched his cheek. "There's much you don't understand. I'll tell you, Gatewood."

"No," he said. "You shouldn't talk any more."

"I've got to talk about it. I've kept it locked up in me so long."

She licked lips that were suddenly dry, and he put the canteen to her mouth again, and she drank.

"The trouble between me and Farrell goes back a while," she began. "It goes back to my husband, my Jim. Farrell caused Jim's death. Jim rode into a lonely cañon and sat down on a rock and put the barrel of his gun into his mouth and pulled the trigger . . . all because of Steve Farrell . . . Farrell's connivings . . . Farrell's big scheme to get Stirrup.

"I didn't catch on to Farrell until after my Jim died. When I did catch on, there was nothing I could do about it. Nobody at Stirrup would believe me. So I got back at Farrell the only way I knew how. I got Wade Stallcup and Red Daniels and Amos Clark and Lonnie Grissom, and we began running off Stirrup stock. I wanted to run off enough beef to make Farrell look bad. That's what I had in mind, but then you came. Gatewood, I don't hate the Renshaws, even though Mister Renshaw drove my Jim away. I've never hated anybody in my life but Steve Farrell, and, as much as I hate him, when I tried to kill him, I failed."

She stopped, exhausted, her chest rising and falling with great, gasping breaths. Then the determination came back into her face, and she went on.

"Maybe you don't believe me, Gatewood, but it's true. Farrell was behind everything that happened to my Jim. He knew that Mister Renshaw didn't approve of Jim's marrying me. So Farrell filled Mister Renshaw with a lot of lies about me, what a cheap hussy I was and how I had married Jim just to get a share of Stirrup. Mister Renshaw kept after Jim either to divorce me or have the marriage annulled. Jim finally was fed up with it and left Stirrup. We got a little spread in the Doloritas and tried to make a go of it there, but Mister Renshaw stopped all our credit in town in the belief that this would drive Jim back to Stirrup. I hated to see Jim suffer like that, and I would have left him, but he loved me too much, and I knew that would have broken his heart, so I stayed with him. Finally he got so discouraged that he rode up that cañon I told you about.

"You see, Gatewood? First Farrell saw to it that Jim left Stirrup. When he left, Mister Renshaw disowned Jim. That left Ellerine to inherit Stirrup. Haven't you noticed how Farrell hangs around that poor girl? No one can so much as look at her without Farrell's beating him up and warning him never to dare look at Ellerine again. He's got her marked down as his. He intends to marry her some day and come into Stirrup that way."

Gatewood nodded. "I understand, Dorcas," he said.

The shadow of death was deep in her eyes. She seemed fully aware of it for her voice took on a pleading urgency. "I know how you feel about me, Gatewood," she whispered, "but it never would have worked out between us. Not that I don't love you. Next to my Jim it would have been you, but never before him or in his place. It's just my Jim for me. So don't cry for me."

Another spasm of pain racked her. Gatewood bent his head and kissed her gently on the lips.

"Thank you, Gatewood," she whispered, and died.

XI

Only one purpose existed in Gatewood now. His mind could grasp nothing but the singularity of this intent. A vicious savagery glowed in his eyes as he scanned the slopes and pitches and escarpments of the Doloritas for some sign of Steve Farrell. Behind Gatewood trailed his grim procession. He had rounded up Dorcas's pinto, and now her dead body was packed across her saddle in the same fashion as Wade Stallcup, Red Daniels, and old Amos Clark were across theirs.

Gatewood had the four horses tethered one to another and then tied to one end of his lariat, the other end of which was looped about his saddle horn.

Gatewood could not get rid of the feeling that Farrell was somewhere about. The man, obsessed with his fanatic rage over the stealing of Stirrup beef, had obviously come into the Doloritas with the cruel purpose of killing the rustlers as he encountered them, in the manner in which he had disposed of young Grissom. Thus Farrell had met Dorcas, as she was emerging from the cañon, and had shot her and left her for dead.

Farrell showed suddenly on top of a sage-and-mesquite-dotted rise. The instant he noticed Gatewood, Farrell reined in his buckskin, staring avidly down the slope at the four horses with their dead burdens.

Gatewood halted the mare, too, the moment he spied Farrell. Swiftly, he loosed the lariat from his saddle horn and then jumped the mare several hops ahead. Farrell had started to come down the slope, but again he reined in his buckskin halfway down the slope.

"That's a nice haul you've got there, Gatewood," he called down jibingly. "I thought you were the boy who was going to bring in the rustlers alive. What made you change your mind? Because they pack better this way?"

Gatewood almost wept with rage. "You yellow-bellied bastard!" he shouted, the cords standing out in his neck. "You dirty, rotten piece of shit!"

"Wait a minute!" Farrell cried. "What have you got to get hot about? You're packing four dead people. What makes you think you're any better than me?"

Wrath hammered in Gatewood's chest and ached behind his eyes. "Three of these dead have nothing to do with it. I'm talking about the fourth one. Understand, Farrell? This is about Dorcas? You knew damn' well who it was. She was still alive, when I found her. She talked to me, Farrell. She told me all about herself and Jim Renshaw and Buck Renshaw and Ellerine and you."

Farrell's eyes were glaring slits. "I've got no idea what she told you, but she always was a cheap, lying hussy. Look, your job is done. I'll be a man, Gatewood, and apologize for all the things I said about you. You've done a hell of a fine job, and me and Stirrup are grateful to you. Why get hot and bothered about it? They were just a bunch of cheap, sneaking rustlers."

Gatewood rose in his stirrups as he shouted: "The devil with Stirrup. The devil with rustlers. The devil with everything else in the world. This is for Dorcas!"

"Don't tempt me, Gatewood. I've never liked you, and I still don't like you, so don't tempt me."

Gatewood settled back in his saddle. His voice was thick with emotion. "All right," he said, "I'll put it this way. You'll never have Stirrup, Farrell. I'm telling Renshaw everything I've found out about you. Then I'm taking Ellerine away from you. You know she can't stand the sight of you."

Farrell lifted a fist and brandished it at Gatewood. "So you think Stirrup will never be mine, do you? What do you think I've worked for all these years? I got rid of Jim Renshaw. I've got the old man in the palm of my hand. That stupid daughter of his will do anything I tell her to. So what's to stop me from getting Stirrup? You, Gatewood? Never! I'm Stirrup. From the day I began ramrodding it, I've been Stirrup, and I'll keep on being Stirrup for a long time after you're dead."

With that, Farrell reached for his gun. He was blindingly fast. Gatewood whipped out his .44, realizing sickeningly that for the first time in his life he had been beaten to the draw. Not by much, but by enough to feel the numbing impact of the slug smashing into him. Still his .44 blasted at the same instant, and then, while the pain began spreading and reeling inside him, he saw Farrell double up over his saddle horn. The buckskin, frightened by the shooting, gave a frantic lunge, and Farrell went toppling out of the kak.

The mare, too, was skittering around, and Gatewood tried to rein her under control, but he didn't have the strength. He felt his mind spinning. The world began to heave crazily about him, and he made a grab for his saddle horn with his left hand, but he missed, and then he was falling.

He hit the ground on his stomach, and for the moment the wind was knocked out of him. The pain was a searing mass in his chest. He gritted his teeth to it, and then began to push himself up enough so that he might see. *Farrell,* the urgency whispered to him. *You've got to be sure about Farrell. You've got to be sure he's dead. . . .*

Gatewood's eyes had cleared enough so that he could see up the slope. Farrell had pulled himself to a sitting position. He was lifting his .45 with both hands. His mouth was pulled down at the corners in a grimace of pain.

He fired. Gatewood felt the bullet burn a searing gash down his back, but by this time he had his .44 lifted again, and he threw a shot up at Farrell. The man emitted a choked grunt and fell over on his side. He began sobbing and snarling through clenched teeth.

"Me, I'm Stirrup. No one's taking Stirrup from me. It's mine. It's mine. Stirrup. Me . . . Steve Farrell . . . I'm Stirrup."

He was pawing and clawing at the ground in his effort to rise. He twisted around finally so that his head pointed down the slope at Gatewood. Then Farrell managed to get his left elbow under him, and with a sobbing, groaning try he raised himself enough so that he could aim his .45 down the hill. He had lost his hat, and his blond hair dangled down in front of his eyes. Angrily, he shook his head to clear his gaze, and the .45 steadied in his hand.

Gatewood fired. Farrell shuddered, and the .45 fell from his lax fingers. He began to cry brokenly. "Stirrup," he sobbed. "Stirrup. Me . . . Steve . . . Farrell . . . I'm . . . Stir. . . ."

Suddenly a gush of blood burst out of his mouth, and he doubled up in a spasm of pain. He cried out loudly, clearly: "Stirrup!" After that, he was still.

Gatewood put his face down on the sand. He could feel the darkness, the comforting blankness coming on, and he was grateful for that. Soon he wouldn't feel anything. He wouldn't remember anything. There would be no more tormenting thoughts. In his last instant of consciousness he thought of Dorcas. At least she was avenged. He had not failed her there.

XII

Two Stirrup riders, having ridden into the Doloritas to look for Farrell when the ramrod had not come into headquarters the night before, found Gatewood. He was unconscious but still alive. The riders fashioned a travois, Indian-style, and brought Gatewood down to Stirrup in that manner.

For a while it was doubtful that Gatewood would pull through, but he rallied and eventually recovered. Ellerine nursed him all the while. It got so that Gatewood felt lonely, when she wasn't around.

The time came for Gatewood to make an explanation.

He had put it off at first with the excuse that he was too ill, but finally he couldn't avoid it any more. He had gone over it in his mind countless times and had finally arrived at the conclusion that it would be best for all concerned, if he changed the facts around a little.

Buck Renshaw and Ellerine were present when Gatewood told about it. He said: "This is how it was. Stallcup, Daniels, Clark, and Grissom were doing the rustling under Farrell's direction. I know you'll find it hard to believe, Renshaw, on the face of certain things, but remember this . . . Farrell was always opposed to having an Association inspector put on the job. Why?

"Sure, he hanged Grissom. The kid was probably tired of it and wanted to quit, and Farrell decided to take no chances on the kid maybe squealing. Besides, by hanging Grissom, Farrell figured on doing away with any suspicion I or anyone else might have had that he was in with the rustlers. When I broke up his gang, he tried to kill me in revenge."

Gatewood paused and his throat tightened. "As for Dorcas, she found out about Farrell, and he killed her to shut her up. She told me that before she died."

He was relieved when the Renshaws accepted this. He had been afraid that Ellerine would see through it, but she gave no indication that she ever suspected the facts were other than as Gatewood had detailed them.

When Gatewood was completely recovered, he and Ellerine rode up the valley to that spot where once he had held her in his arms. For a while now Gatewood had been fighting with himself. He felt that he was straightened out as far as Dorcas was concerned. He would never forget her. She had meant too much to him ever to be forgotten. But he had come to realize the truth of those last words she had spoken to him. It never would have worked out between them. Dorcas's love had been totally for Jim Renshaw. Thus it was that he felt he could say what he wanted to say to Ellerine.

"I'll be leaving soon," he said. "I've worked for the Association for five years, and now I'm tired of it. I'm tired of drifting, of being beat up and shot at, of prying into things that sometimes almost destroy my faith in human beings. I've saved a little money, and I'd like to get a small ranch and settle down. Would you come with me, Ellerine?"

Tears came into her eyes, and she nodded eagerly. "But why leave Stirrup?" she asked.

"I want to marry you, but not because of Stirrup. I want to prove that to you."

"Are you starting that, too? Am I supposed to become an old maid just because some day I'll inherit a rich ranch? Do you think I'd ever marry you, if I felt that was what you had in mind? That's why I hated Steve Farrell. I knew he didn't care about me. He only wanted to marry me so he could get Stirrup."

He smiled and pulled her up against him. She rested her head against his chest and said: "I'd go anywhere with you, but it's Dad. He needs me. He's all alone. I can't leave him here helpless and with all those memories of Jim and Dorcas. I know it's a little easier on him, after what you said about Dorcas. He always suspected her of being behind the rustling to get even for Jim. You don't know how grateful I am for what you told him."

Gatewood held her closer and stroked her hair. He lifted his eyes and looked up at the rugged heights of the Doloritas. As he stared, he promised himself that until the day he died he would keep that secret — between just him and Dorcas.

H(enry) A(ndrew) DeRosso was born on July 15, 1917 in Carey, Wisconsin. This area, in the northeast corner of the state near the Michigan border, is rich in its own pioneer history. Carey and its neighboring community of Hurley in which DeRosso made his home for many years were once rough-and-tumble iron-ore mining towns not unlike the gold, silver, and copper camps of the Far West frontier. This rural milieu, with its harsh winters and its proximity to the vast North Woods, may explain DeRosso's early interest in adventure and Western fiction and his lifelong fascination with the southwestern desert country, a wilderness and a climate exactly opposite of the one in which he lived. He began producing Western short stories while a high-school student, making his first professional sale to Street & Smith's *Western Story Magazine* in 1941. Health problems kept him out of military service during World War II, and thus he was able to continue writing on a daily basis and to begin piling up sales to *Western Story* and other pulps during this period, supplementing his income with farm work and as a mail carrier. By the end of the war he had established himself to the point where he was able to devote his full time to writing. Nearly all of his tales are set in the stark, desolate wastes of the Southwest. In the decades between 1940 and 1960 he published appoximately two hundred Western short stories and short novels in various pulp magazines that became known for their dark and compelling visions of the night side of life and their austere realism. He was also the author of six western novels, perhaps the most enjoyable of which are *.44* (1953) and *End of the Gun* (1955). He died on October 14, 1960. His most recently-published short stories include *Under the Burning Sun* (1997) and *Riders of the Shadowlands* (1999).

Bill Pronzini was born in Petaluma, California. His earliest Western fiction was the short story, *Sawtooth Justice,* published in *Zane Grey Western Magazine* (11/69). A number of short stories followed before he published his first Western novel, *The Gallows Land* (1983), which has the same beginning as the story, *Decision,* but with the rider, instead, returning to the Todd ranch. Although Pronzini has earned an enviable reputation as an author of detective stories, he has continued periodically to write Western novels, most notably perhaps *Starvation Camp* (1984) and *Firewind* (1989) as well as Western short stories. Over the years he has also edited a great number of Western fiction anthologies and single-author Western story collections. Most recently these have included *Under The Burning Sun: Western Stories* (1997) by H.A. DeRosso, *Renegade River: Western Stories* (1998) by Giff Cheshire, *Riders Of The Shadowlands: Western Stories* (1999) by H.A. DeRosso, and *Heading West: Western Stories* (1999) by Noel M. Loomis. In his own Western stories, Pronzini has tended toward narratives that avoid excessive violence and, instead, are character studies in which a person has to deal with personal flaws or learn to live with the consequences of previous actions. As an editor and anthologist, Pronzini has demonstrated both rare éclat and reliable good taste in selecting very fine stories by other authors, fiction notable for its human drama and memorable characters. He is married to author Marcia Muller, who has written Western stories as well as detective stories, and even occasionally collaborated with her husband on detective novels. They make their home in Petaluma, California.

All stories were edited by Bill Pronzini for publication in this collection.